SURVIVING

HIGH

SCHOOL

SURVIVING HIGH SCHOOL

A NOVEL BY M. DOTY

poppy

LITTLE, BROWN AND COMPANY

New York Boston

Poppy

Hachette Book Group
237 Park Avenue, New York, NY 10017
For more of your favorite series and novels, visit our website at www.pickapoppy.com

Poppy is an imprint of Little, Brown and Company.
The Poppy name and logo are trademarks of Hachette Book Group, Inc.

The publisher is not responsible for websites (or their content) that are not owned by the publisher.

First Edition: September 2012

ISBN 978-0-316-22015-6

10 9 8 7 6 5 4 3 2 1

RRD-C

Printed in the United States of America

TO MY MOTHER AND FATHER

PROLOGUE

The sky was so thick with rain that the tiny Honda might as well have been driving underwater. It was May, not too long before school would be out, and early for a summer storm. Water seeped into cracks in the asphalt, and multicolored oil slicks floated everywhere. The driver didn't see them.

Coming around a corner, the car skidded off the road and over a steep embankment. From there, it tumbled onto its side, flipping twice before it landed in a small, grassy stream below.

For a moment, everything was still except for the falling rain. Then came the sound of crunching glass as a boot kicked out the windshield from inside. A tall boy with a deep gash across his face crawled from the wreckage, dragging a girl behind him. She didn't move, didn't even breathe.

"Sara!" the boy shouted, holding his face close to hers, hoping he'd feel her breath. He did not, and he shouted her name again. Then he pressed his lips to hers and exhaled, trying to breathe life back into her.

But even before the ambulances came, before the men tore him away from her and put him on a stretcher, even before Sara's father arrived and stared coldly down at him, cursing him for what he'd done, the boy knew that she was dead.

CHAPTER
ONE

"Smile."

Emily Kessler willed the corners of her mouth to rise and her eyes to light up as she stared into the massive camera lens. If her photo turned out like usual, she'd be stuck with a miserable school ID card all year. She hadn't looked happy in a picture in months.

Smile, she thought. *Smile.*

"Uh, great. Hold it just like that," said the photographer, scrambling to find the button on his camera. Emily's mouth was starting to hurt.

"Just one more second—"

Forget it, she thought. *I'm doomed.*

By the time the flash went off a few seconds later, she was wearing her usual intense expression: awesome for scaring the Speedos off the other swimmers during a meet, terrible for trying to make friends...or meet a cute guy.

A few seconds later, the photographer apologized as he handed Emily her new ID.

"I usually don't say this," he said, "but if you 'lose' this after a few weeks, they'll send you back here to get another one."

"Thanks," she said, accepting the card. She knew there'd be no point in taking him up on his offer.

Out in the hallway, a line of other freshmen stretched into the distance and around a corner. Rows and rows of endless lockers went on as far as the eye could see, and Emily wondered which one was hers. She squinted at the sheet of paper the school had mailed her a few days earlier. Locker 1322? The number itself seemed overwhelming. Her middle school had only had six hundred students, less than half the number here at Twin Branches High.

The students in line smiled, laughed, chewed gum, read over their schedules, chatted, and flirted. Emily watched them nervously. How could they possibly look so happy and calm?

Somewhere, in one of these halls, Nick Brown was walking around, looking for his first class and getting ready to start his senior year. Nick Brown was here. And Sara wasn't. It just didn't seem fair. How could the world be like this, where you got a girl killed and then just showed up at school the next year as if everything was normal?

Emily still didn't understand how it had happened, really.

Sara almost always walked or jogged home from school. Given the storm that night, she might have decided to get a ride, but why hadn't she just called their parents? To ride home with some random guy from school—that wasn't Sara's style.

The first few days after Sara's death were a black hole in Emily's memory. Whatever Emily had thought or felt back then, it was simply gone. A week went by before she'd had the courage to ask her parents about the details of what had happened.

She'd walked into her dad's office one evening to find him sitting in a chair and staring at the screen of a laptop that had gone into standby mode.

"Dad," she'd said, "why did she ride home with him—with Nick Brown?"

The mention of the boy's name had made her father cringe.

"Your sister made a stupid mistake," he said.

"But why did she—"

"Emily, enough!"

He turned his attention back to his computer then, clicking it awake, and Emily had stood stupidly in the doorway, watching him type for a few moments before retreating to the solitude of her room. Emily's father had always been intense, but something had changed in him after the accident, as if any joy he took in life had died along with Sara.

And for all this, she had Nick Brown to thank.

Just thinking about him made Emily's throat constrict

and her chest burn. Who knew what would happen if she actually saw him? The best she could hope for was to make it through the next year without bumping into him. Yeah, right. Twin Branches High School was big—but it probably wasn't *that* big.

As Emily turned to start looking for her first class, her best friend, Kimi Chen, ran up and snatched the freshly printed ID out of Emily's hands. They looked down at the photo together: Emily's brown hair was pulled back tight, and the flash shone off her forehead like it was a giant Ping-Pong ball. The worst thing was that her eyes, which were supposed to be blue, instead glowed crimson. The whole look was completely terrifying. Didn't the school's camera have red-eye reduction?

"Scary!" said Kimi, wrinkling her nose. "You totally look like that girl who gets possessed by a demon in that movie. You know, the one where the priest gets thrown out the window?"

"Great," said Emily, snatching back the ID and burying it in her jeans pocket. "I've always wanted to look like a movie star."

Emily gave Kimi a once-over. Kimi had styled her usually straight black hair into waves, and she wore a brown pencil skirt with a crisp white collared shirt and black wedges. Maybe a little formal for high school, but it was the first day. Lots of people dressed up. The whitening strips Kimi had been applying all summer made her teeth sparkle like snow and matched the single pearl she wore around her neck.

"You look—nice," said Emily.

"It's business casual," said Kimi, smiling coyly. "First impressions count for everything, and the teachers here need to know who they're dealing with. I'm going for a studious-yet-highly-efficient, sexy-secretary kind of look. What do you think?"

Two girls in the nearby line laughed a little too loudly, and Emily and Kimi turned to find out what was so funny. It took a moment for Emily to recognize Dominique Clark and Lindsay Vale without their swim caps on. Great. Two *more* people she'd hoped to avoid today.

"Nice outfit, Chen," said Dominique. "Let me guess. You're here to sell real estate?"

Kimi blushed and looked down at her skirt.

"This is vintage!"

"You mean 'old,'" said Dominique, smiling icily.

"Don't be so hard on her," added Lindsay. "At least her clothes *fit*." She glared over at Emily's baggy jeans and too-big sweatshirt. The clothes were hand-me-downs from Sara that Emily had dug out of a box in the garage a week earlier. She knew how loose they were, and her mom had offered to take her shopping, but Emily refused to wear anything else.

Kimi stared the blondes down, trying to melt them with her eyes. Both of them wore pastel summer dresses and had obviously visited the salon in the last twenty-four hours: Their shimmering platinum hair was as artfully arranged as Japanese flowers. Dominique and Lindsay didn't look good— they looked *perfect*.

After a second, Kimi smiled.

"At least Emily and I aren't wearing the same *shoes*," she said, pointing at their feet. Dominique and Lindsay looked down in horror. It was true. They were wearing the same designer ballet flats.

"Hope you had a nice summer, Emily," said Dominique, quickly recovering. "I noticed you didn't make it down to LA for training camp. Too bad. All the other girls were asking about you."

"My dad—Coach—thought it would be better for my form if I just trained here," said Emily, gritting her teeth. "Fewer distractions."

"Oh, he's *totally* right," said Dominique, twirling her hair around a finger, her French-tipped nail cutting through the air. "We ended up having to go to these awful parties with Michael Phelps and some of the other guys from the Olympic team. *So* boring. I'm sure you were better off here at Twin Branches with Coach. I can't *wait* to start working with him again."

"Come on, Emily," Kimi said. "Let's get out of here."

"See you at the pool!" Dominique called as Kimi dragged Emily away from the blondes and down the hall.

"Stupid name-dropper," said Kimi once they were out of earshot, her face flushed with rage. "She's not even that good of a swimmer."

"Yes, she is," admitted Emily.

"Okay, fine. But not as good as you—right?"

Emily had checked Dominique's summer race times

8

online, and they'd been almost identical to her own. Over the last two years, ever since Dominique had moved to town to work with Emily's dad as part of a club sport back in middle school, the two girls had gone head-to-head dozens of times, with Emily dominating in breaststroke and butterfly and Dominique beating her in freestyle and backstroke.

"We'll see," said Emily. "It's a new year."

Kimi reached into her bag, took out a meticulously organized notebook, and flipped to the inside cover, where she'd taped her class schedule.

"Who do you have for homeroom?" she asked.

"Ms. Prez."

"Shoot. I've got Sanderson."

Emily glanced over Kimi's schedule.

"So we don't have homeroom together," she said, frowning as she read the list. "Or anything else. Aren't you in *any* honors classes?"

"Not this year," said Kimi. "It's all about strategy. Back in middle school, when I tried to step it up and take all those gifted classes with you, I got mostly B's and C's. I figure if I just take the regular stuff, I can pull off straight A's. Good for the résumé and good enough for my parents. Plus, I'll probably have way more time after school for, you know, 'activities.' "

Emily arched an eyebrow.

"I thought you stopped going to that hip-hop dance class."

"Some people's bones just aren't made to pop and lock, okay? I was *actually* thinking something more along the lines of flirting with hot guys at the mall," said Kimi. "You want to head over there after school?"

"I wish I could. But, you know, swimming. Besides, I don't have time for guys. I barely have time to text back and forth with *you*."

"*Everyone* has time for guys," said Kimi. "I mean, come on! Homecoming is only, like, two and a half months away. Then there's the winter formal two months after that. Not to mention prom in eight months—and that means getting a junior or senior to invite you. We're practically behind schedule already!"

Emily laughed.

"Me at a dance? You're kidding, right? You *have* met my dad." It was true that Emily's dad had set an outright ban on her dating, much less going to dances, until she was in college. Not that it really mattered: Between school, swim practice, and homework, Emily's schedule was booked for the next four years anyway.

"Your dad, huh?" Kimi asked. "I just thought that now that we're in high school, you might want to stop living like a nun."

"I have a great system with guys," said Emily. "I don't have time for them, and they're not interested in me."

"Sounds to me like you just haven't met the right one," said Kimi. "But we'll work on that."

"Okay," said Emily, eager to end the conversation. "I'd better get to class—if I can find it."

Kimi looked over Emily's schedule and wrinkled her brow.

"Hm...room 246B? That's probably on the second floor of the library building. Too bad. It looks like we're going in opposite directions. I'm headed down that hall over there."

"Our homerooms aren't even in the same *building*?" Emily felt a wave of panic rising in her.

"Relax," said Kimi. "There's a map on the back of your schedule. Just follow that and you'll be fine."

Unfortunately, Emily's journey to room 246B proved to be slightly more perilous than Kimi had predicted. Emily was halfway across the parking lot when she realized she'd been holding her map upside down and had to circle back. By that time, the first bell of the day had rung, and the halls were mostly empty.

Once she got to the library building, Emily's luck didn't get much better. The signs indicating where each classroom was located were all outdated, missing, or simply wrong, and she was forced to check every door, hoping she'd finally find the right one.

She was beginning to think she'd never get to room 246B when she bumped into a pretty redheaded girl dressed in a knee-length black skirt with matching leggings and a white tailored blouse. Rather than a backpack, the girl carried an elegant black leather handbag. Maybe Kimi's first-day outfit wasn't as out of place as Emily had thought.

"You look almost as lost as I am," said the redhead. "Which room are you looking for?"

"246B."

"Well, then we're both in the same boat," said the girl, offering her hand. "I'm Alicia, by the way."

"I'm Emily." Given Alicia's sophisticated clothes and bag, Emily would never have pegged her for a fellow lost freshman. "Are you, like, a transfer or something?"

Alicia smiled. "Something like that. Come on," she added. "I think we're almost there."

Sure enough, Emily and Alicia found their classroom a few doors down. As they walked inside, Emily turned to Alicia and asked, "Want to sit together?"

Alicia smiled again. "Unfortunately, I can't."

Can't? thought Emily as she took a seat near the front of the room. Then, as she settled into her chair and looked up, she saw Alicia walk up to the whiteboard and write her full name: ALICIA PREZ.

"Apologies for my tardiness," Alicia said, turning back to the class. "They've literally moved my classroom four times in the last week as we've been getting ready for the new year. Trust me when I say that I arrived thirty minutes early in 246A."

The other students in the class chuckled as Emily cringed. She couldn't believe it. One class in, and she'd already completely embarrassed herself in front of her teacher. *Are you, like, a transfer or something?* She slunk low in her chair as if trying to hide from Alicia's gaze.

12

"Now," said Alicia, "a few ground rules for homeroom. One, you are permitted to call me Alicia or Ms. Prez, depending on your personal preference. Two, this is *your* homeroom—the place where you come to check in, tell me how you're doing, and complain about your other classes. Juicy gossip on the rest of the faculty is appreciated and even welcomed. It's my first year here, so I'm going to need all the ammunition I can get."

"Do you have a boyfriend?!" someone shouted from the back of the classroom, and Alicia's eyes suddenly went cold.

"Right. Number three: I may look like some starry-eyed innocent fresh out of grad school, but allow me to assure you that this kitty has fangs. Any more comments like that, and you may just find yourself transferred to homeroom with Mr. Upton—*his* first class of the year always starts with an informative scared-straight talk with some very nice felons who I'm sure would *love* to meet you."

There wasn't another peep out of the class.

"Excellent," said Alicia. "I just know this is going to be an awesome year."

The girl next to Emily turned to a black-haired guy behind her and whispered, "I want to *be* her."

Emily couldn't help but agree.

The rest of the morning passed smoothly. Almost too smoothly. Since Emily's run-in with Dominique and Lindsay that morning, no one bothered her about her clothes, her hair, or her stupid ID. In fact, no one paid attention to her at all. She kept an eye out for Nick Brown, but because he was a senior, it was unlikely they'd share any classes. She just had to be on alert in the hallways during period changes.

In Geometry, Emily breezed through the practice problems that Mr. Gibbs presented as "a taste of what's to come," but she didn't make a big deal about finishing them in five minutes like Deependu Mahajan or Eric Erickson. She sat in the back, calmly checking her work until Mr. Gibbs announced the answers.

In English, she tried to talk to Bryce Holmgren, Tony Kan, and a couple of the other guys she knew from the swim team, but after a quick hello they turned around and started chatting up Linda Byrne and Paula de Veer, whose mouths shimmered with lip gloss.

"You going to Ben Kale's place this Friday?" Tony asked the girls. "His parties are supposed to be legendary."

"Ben Kale? I thought he got expelled last year," said Paula.

"Just suspended," said Tony. "He's totally back with a vengeance."

"You think you can get us into his party?" asked Linda.

"For sure," said Tony. "Hot girls are always welcome."

Paula and Linda giggled, blushed, and said they'd "think about it," which meant they'd definitely be there. The guys didn't bother inviting Emily, not that she could go anyway. *Still*, she thought, *they could have at least asked.*

As she went from class to class, Emily felt like a visitor, an impostor, a middle schooler, or a narc trying unsuccessfully to infiltrate the high school. She stared at the older girls' dark skinny jeans or short dresses and at their arms wrapped around boyfriends in varsity jackets.

In an attempt to reassure herself, she tried to count the other girls wearing sneakers, but they seemed just as lost as she was, shuffling through the halls with their eyes on the gray tiled floor, holding their books tight against their chests, darting right and left to avoid physical contact—especially with guys.

CHAPTER TWO

At lunch, Emily sat with Kimi at a table in a corner of the cafeteria, where she would be able to spot Nick Brown or Dominique before they noticed her. Most tables at the edges of the cafeteria were either uninhabited or populated by pockets of nerds and outcasts, scrubby skaters, and geeks with long white boxes of gaming cards.

At the table to the left of Kimi and Emily, a pair of boys as pale as vampires rolled dice and pretended they were medieval warriors. One wore a T-shirt that read GAME GEEK across the chest. His questionably cooler friend had a Spider-Man backpack.

The next layer of tables in was filled with band and drama geeks who weren't necessarily popular but formed a large-enough contingent that no one messed with them. Then there were the preps, the dumber jocks, some of the more clean-cut skaters and punks, and the cooler half of the emo crowd—kids on the edge of popularity. And just past them, deep in the heart of the cafeteria, was the center table.

To understand the center table meant viewing Twin Branches High as a solar system. The nerds inhabited the icy asteroids on the farthest reaches. Then, as you got closer to the middle, the planets became larger, warmer, and more desirable—until finally you reached the sun, the bright center, the spot where only the most popular kids dared to sit: the center table.

The center table stood in the middle of the cafeteria beneath a massive skylight that bathed it in intense sunbeams, even on cloudy days. Unlike the long picnic-style tables that made up most of the cafeteria's furniture, the center table was circular and surrounded by an elegant, curved bench. Seating was limited, and upperclassmen tended to take up most of the space, but Dominique and Lindsay sat there flashing their perfect smiles at the cute boys who surrounded them. Emily tried not to look.

"Let me guess, a dark elf thief and a human cleric?" asked a small, plump, dark-skinned boy from the table to their right. "I can always spot fellow gamers."

"I don't—um, steal things," said Emily, slightly confused.

"Forgive Amir," said a tall, lanky guy with a serious computer tan and wearing a Batman T-shirt. "He's not used to conversations with actual females. We were just curious if you want to sit with us—since we're stuck together here in the outer reaches, you know? I'm Kevin, by the way. Kevin Delucca."

"Uh, sure—" Emily started, before Kimi cut her off.

"Actually, we have some private matters to discuss," she said.

As the boys returned to their game, Emily leaned over and whispered to Kimi, "What's up with you? They seemed like nice guys."

"Emily, Emily, Emily. Don't be so naïve. Right now, as *fresh*men, we're a fresh commodity here. Sure, we're not popular *yet*, but I'd like to think that one day we could be. If we start hanging out with guys like that, it's never going to happen. We'll be branded nerd girls for life."

"Okay," said Emily, though she didn't quite buy the logic. "I'm too hungry to talk much anyway."

While Kimi sat beside her nibbling on half a bagel and some cottage cheese, Emily pulled out her lunch: yogurt, a whey protein shake, orange juice, half a loaf of whole-wheat bread smeared with almond butter, Muscle Milk, a tin of almonds, a sack of vitamins, raisins, two bananas, and a package of thin-sliced turkey. Laid out in front of her, the food took up almost a third of their cafeteria table. Luckily, no one else was sitting with them.

"You sure you don't want a couple of pizzas to go with that?" asked Kimi, her eyes big.

"I guess I'm not that hungry," said Emily, smiling. "I had a big breakfast."

"I bet you did," said Kimi, savoring half a spoonful of cottage cheese. "How many calories a day are you up to now?"

"Eight thousand. But you should see the *guy* swimmers eat. I mean, most people don't regulate their percentages of carbs, proteins, and fats correctly. You'd be surprised how even at the Olympic level a lot of the guys are just eating deep-fried turkeys and cheese sandwiches. Some of them eat, like, twelve thousand or thirteen thousand calories a day, which is probably on the high end of what they should be—"

"Oh yeah," interrupted Kimi. "*That* would be a lot. I mean, eight thousand calories is barely anything—for a *polar bear*. It's so unfair. If I even eat, like, two extra cookies, my jeans don't fit anymore. My mom says our family has slow metab—"

"Eat! Eat! Eat! Eat!"

At the center table, a group of junior and senior guys had formed a circle around Dominique and were shouting encouragement as she ate. She actually *was* wolfing down two pizzas. As she got to the last couple of slices, the guys continued chanting: "Dominique! Dominique!"

Emily rolled her eyes. *Show-off.* Dominique had been hanging out with older kids—especially guys—ever since she'd come to town. Her older half brother, Cameron, swam for the guys' team, providing Dominique with an easy introduction to many of his teammates, who were among the most popular guys at school.

Cameron himself was more of a loner, a strong swimmer with a near-perfect body that left girls tripping over their own tongues. Even Emily, who heard barely any gossip, knew he'd dated half of the popular girls and hooked up with the rest.

Today, he sat watching Dominique's performance with a wry smile, even as his friends cheered her on.

As Dominique finished the last slice, the crowd applauded and held up the empty pizza boxes for the rest of the cafeteria to see. A couple of the guys peeled off from the crowd and walked away, talking to each other. One was huge, his tight blue T-shirt straining to contain his bulky muscles. He also had the worst haircut in the world: a terrible buzz cut with the words GO LIZARDS shaved into the back, stretching from ear to ear.

The other boy, though, was gorgeous. He wore a red-and-white-striped polo shirt that hung loose, except for the sleeves, which clung to his well-toned arms. His dark brown hair fell just over eyes that sparkled with intelligence. Emily bet he had a nice smile, too, but he wasn't smiling now.

"Dude, a hot chick who can pack away that much pizza is basically a goddess," said the bigger one, whose letterman jacket read SPENCER on the chest. "I'm all over that."

"Yeah," the hot one said without enthusiasm. "Sure."

"You okay, man?" Spencer put a hand on his friend's shoulder. "You seem—I dunno—off, or something."

"Just bored. One day back and I'm already bored. Maybe there *is* something wrong with me. I just can't get excited about a girl putting away two pizzas."

"Are you crazy?" asked Spencer. "Dominique is basically the perfect woman. She's like a guy—but in an incredibly hot girl's body. And did you hear that she watches every NFL game on Sundays while she runs on the treadmill—for six hours? I started fantasizing about her listing quarterback ratings while she wrestled me to the ground and—"

"Okay, okay, I get it," said his friend. "But can you imagine going on dates? She'd totally empty your wallet every time you went out for dinner. I'll stick to girls who only want a slice or two."

"Whatever, man," said Spencer. "I still say she's hot. I could see her perfect abs *through her dress*! Where did she even *put* those pizzas?"

The guys began walking toward the door, on a path that would take them right past Emily and Kimi's table. Emily instinctively looked down, preparing herself to avoid eye contact, and then she remembered the banquet she'd laid out for herself. *I'll stick to girls who only want a slice or two.* Great. This guy clearly wasn't going to be impressed by her megacalorie meal. Now the only boy in the world she actually thought was hot (besides Taylor Lautner, maybe) was going to think she was just as high maintenance as Dominique.

"Kimi!" she said, trying to keep her voice down. "Help!"

"Help what?"

Emily picked the bread and turkey off the table and laid them on the bench by her side. She reached for her vitamins next. Catching on, Kimi picked up the almonds and set the can in her lap.

Emily was reaching forward, trying to hide one more thing when the guys walked by, and she tried to sneak a glance at the cute one. As he passed, a strong scent filled her nostrils, something like a combination of vanilla and

21

chocolate chip cookies. Emily couldn't believe it: She was literally salivating over a guy.

Suddenly, the boys stopped. Right in front of Emily and Kimi's table. Emily tried to act like she'd been looking at something over the guys' shoulders.

"Uh, hey. Are you okay?" asked the cute one.

Emily looked up to confirm that, yes, he was *actually* talking to her. He had a confused look on his face, but she detected the faintest hint of a smile arcing up at the side of his mouth.

"I'm—fine," she finally said.

"It's just"—he glanced down at the table—"you have your hand in a bowl of yogurt."

Emily looked down and saw that what he'd said was true.

"Oh. That's. Yes. That's, uh. I burned my hand on—a beaker. In Chemistry. And the yogurt is supposed to help the skin heal."

The guys stood silent for a second, looking at her. Then the cute one broke out into a big full-faced smile that reached all the way up to his eyes.

"Chemistry, huh?" he said. Then he turned and left, laughing a little to himself as he and Spencer walked out the side door. Emily took her fingers out of the yogurt and wiped them off on a napkin. Perfect. Now the rest of the container would taste like her hand—meaning it would taste like chlorine. Maybe she could make up the yogurt calories at dinner.

"I can't believe it," said Kimi, putting the almonds back on the table. "You were just talking to Ben Kale!"

Emily spent the rest of the day in constant alert mode. Now she had three people to avoid at all costs: Nick, Dominique—and Ben Kale. Not that she would *hate* to see him again, but the thought of running into him in the hall and having him ask about her "injured" hand filled her with enough embarrassment to send a shiver down her back.

At least her classes didn't seem too hard—that was, until she got to her last one of the day: Honors History, where the teacher, Mr. McBride, gleefully handed out thick "supplementary" textbooks to the entire class. Mr. McBride was a tall, wiry man, towering over the students. He was Ping-Pong–ball bald, but he made up for it with two extremely bushy eyebrows whose gray hairs seemed to stick out as far as a cat's whiskers.

"Technically, the administration has deemed this textbook too difficult for first-year students," he said, pacing the room and slamming the books down one by one on the students' desks. "They even went so far as to ban the library from passing them out to Twin Branches students. Luckily, I have a friend at a used bookstore who picked me up my own personal set for pennies on the dollar. But be warned! There are no replacement copies. Lose your book, and I dock you a letter grade. Worse than that, though, you won't have a book to read. Get the message? Hold on to this book as if your very life depends on it! In many ways, it does."

Mr. McBride got to Emily's desk and slammed her textbook down. Her heart skipped several beats as he glowered down at her and said, "Welcome to Honors History." Then he

23

turned on one foot, took two monumental steps toward his dry-erase board, and shouted, "Lesson one: the Fertile Crescent!"

Emily took a deep breath, trying to slow her heartbeat. Why hadn't she just taken regular classes with Kimi? Emily carefully opened the book, trying to make sure she didn't so much as bend a page.

It wasn't until after school, when she'd changed into her swim gear and walked into the gym housing the indoor pool, that the tension drained from Emily's body and she felt at peace. The deep chlorine scent of the water filled the air, and the tight fabric of her swimsuit hugged her like a long-lost sister.

She got up on one of the blocks and stared down the length of the pool. Official practices during the fall semester were on Mondays and Thursdays. Right now, the rest of the girls on the team would be in their living rooms, snacking and watching MTV or texting their friends about which guys had gotten cuter over the summer. The gym was empty, the water perfectly smooth. Emily felt like a mermaid returning home: Over the past few years, she had probably spent as much time in the water as out of it.

The smooth grain of the white block tickled the undersides of her feet as she rocked slightly back and forth, readying her body for the wet shock of the water. She leaned forward and bent her knees to get into the forward-start position.

She imagined the announcer's voice echoing through the gym: "Three...Two...One..." And then the horn.

Emily dove forward, slicing through the water. She came up a third of the way down the lane and reached forward with both hands, pulling her head up for air. She did the breast-stroke down the length of the pool, touched the wall with both hands, and pushed off again, kicking once underwater, the way Sara had shown her.

Sara's nickname had been "the Machine," and it fit her well: Her mechanics were perfect. She'd shown Emily how to look for the overhead flags when she did the backstroke to gauge how long she had until she hit the wall and the way to breathe on every other stroke in freestyle to maximize her oxygen flow.

Their father had liked Sara's nickname. "Girls don't win gold medals," he'd say. "Machines do." And when Emily would ask to go to the mall with Kimi, her dad would remind her of it, telling her, "Just ask any swimmer who's ever stood on the podium how many parties she's gone to, what her favorite stand at the food court is, how many boyfriends she's had. She'll look at you like you're nuts. Those are things you do when you're too old to win anymore."

Emily went back and forth for several laps at 75 percent effort and kept swimming well beyond the length of an actual race. As she felt the cool water slide over her skin, the stresses of the day—the bad picture, the confrontation with Dominique, learning that she shared no classes with Kimi, embarrassing herself in front of Ben, and Mr. McBride's supplemental textbook—escaped her body and dissolved into the water.

The only thing she couldn't quite shake was her fear of seeing Nick Brown. Even now, she half expected to pop out of the water and find him staring down at her from the side of the pool. The last time she'd seen him had been at the hospital, when he'd tried to get in to see Sara's body. Black stitches had lined the bridge of his nose, and both of his eyes had been bruised purple in the crash. When she imagined running into him in the hallways here, she still saw him like that—cut, bruised, and shaken, barely alive.

But when Emily pulled up her goggles and rested her arms over the side of the pool, it wasn't Nick Brown she saw but rather her father, sitting on one of the blocks, his legs dangling above the water. His paunch stuck out over his too-tight pants, and his dark beard couldn't cover up his fast-growing double chin. Looking at him, you'd barely recognize the guy who'd shocked the world by winning the Olympic gold medal for the butterfly in '84. Even a few years ago he'd still been trim, swimming in the mornings—but not anymore. Emily wondered how long he'd been watching her.

"Why are you in your race gear?" he asked. "We bought you that resistance suit for a reason. You've got to build muscle or you're never going to lower your split times."

"It's my first day here. I just want to relax."

"And you think Dominique is relaxing in that big indoor pool her parents built her? Or Chelsea Wong? Or Kate—"

"Fine. Fine, Dad. I'll change."

"Coach," he said. "You'll call me Coach while we're at school. Just like the other girls." She nodded. At least she didn't have any actual classes with him. Although the school had hired him for his proficiency as a coach, district policy dictated that he had to teach at least two classes. He had ended up teaching two juniors-only courses in Family Health, which included such topics as nutrition, stress management, and—most disturbing—sex ed.

He looked down at Emily resting, and she reflexively pulled off the pool's edge and started treading water. "One other thing—I almost forgot. A reporter from *Swimmer's Monthly* is coming by in a couple of weeks to do a story on you and Dominique. It's a chance to get your name out there, and it's good practice for later. Unfortunately, part of being an athlete of your caliber means dealing with the press."

Emily frowned. The swimming she could handle. Reporters were a different matter. Not that she had a choice. She tried to make eye contact with her dad, but he looked away from her, up at a list of names and times on the wall of the gym:

MARION KNOWLES, 50M FREESTYLE, 25.45

STACEY JACKSON, 100M FREESTYLE, 58.22

And there, in the bottom right-hand corner:

SARA KESSLER, 50M BACKSTROKE, 28.30

In fact, Sara's name appeared in several places across the board, but it was the 50-meter-backstroke time that truly mattered—not just a school record, but a national one for high schoolers. The mark had stood for almost a year now. Most impressive, Sara had set it as only a sophomore.

"You're on the right track," Emily's father said as he got to his feet and hopped off the block. "Stick with your training program, and you could own every record on that board." He looked again at the wall of names, and Emily could tell which one he was concentrating on. "Now get to the locker room and put on your resistance gear. We've only got two hours before this place shuts down."

A couple of hours to go—and then a four-mile run to get home. Not that Emily minded. Better a thirty-minute jog than getting in the car. Better than the panicked feeling of strapping on her seat belt and feeling her stomach lurch as her dad started the engine.

For almost a month after Sara's accident, Emily had refused to even sit in a car. She'd ridden her bike to school, refused trips to movie theaters that were too far away to walk to, and insisted her family cancel their annual road trip to SeaWorld.

Eventually, she'd relented and started letting her father drive her around when it was absolutely necessary, reassuring herself that he'd never been in an accident and consistently went five miles per hour under the speed limit, much to the displeasure of other drivers.

Still, she wished the whole world could just be a pool, with people swimming from place to place. It could be like Venice, with men in silly hats pushing their gondolas down canals instead of streets. Emily wouldn't have minded getting in a boat: Those hardly ever wrecked, right? *Titanic* was, like, a hundred years ago.

A boat never went so fast that a crash would kill you. A boat rocked gently on the waves, putting you to sleep. A boat would never have spun out of control because some stupid teenage boy was at the wheel.

CHAPTER THREE

It wasn't until the second week of school that Emily bumped into Nick Brown.

At lunch on Monday, as Emily entered the cafeteria and began walking to what had become her usual spot in the corner, she noticed Dominique and Lindsay sitting in the no-man's-land between the band geeks and the wrestling-team jocks. The two girls were leaning close to each other, whispering and giggling. Whatever they were talking about must have been top secret—and important enough that they'd leave their usual spot at the center table in order to get some privacy.

Emily altered her route through the cafeteria so that it would take her right behind the girls. When she neared them, she slowed her pace, both so that they wouldn't hear her footsteps and to have more time to overhear them. As she approached, Emily distinctly heard Lindsay say "Ben Kale." Emily slowed to a glacial pace, but it was no use: A few more steps and she'd be out of listening range.

To her right was an empty table, close enough that she'd hear everything. But could she really risk occupying a random table all by herself? She looked around the cafeteria, hoping to find Kimi and summon her over, but couldn't spot her anywhere.

"Come on. What happened to you at the party Friday?" Lindsay whispered. "It was, like, one second I was pouring you a drink, then the next, *poof.* You and Ben were gone."

There was no choice. Emily had to hear this. She sat with her back to Dominique and Lindsay and prayed that they wouldn't notice her. She pulled a bag of almonds out of her backpack. Her new strategy was to eat one food item at a time in order to avoid a repeat of the yogurt incident.

"And then you didn't respond to *one* text all weekend?" continued Lindsay. "*Tell me* you made out with Ben and ran off to Vegas to get married."

Emily bit down a little too hard on an almond, and a burst of pain filled her jaw as her teeth knocked against each other. The thought of Dominique putting her tongue in Ben's mouth made her want to either cry or gag. Possibly both.

"I wish," said Dominique. "I was *totally* ready to jump him when we got to the bedroom. But then Spencer was waiting there!"

Emily's shoulders relaxed a little. *Thank you, Spencer.*

31

"Spencer?" Lindsay asked. "As in 'Go Lizards' Spencer?"

"I don't get why Ben is friends with that guy. *Such* a tool."

"Yeah. He's definitely a fixer-upper and a half. His body's not so bad, though. If you like, you know, bodybuilder-type guys—"

"Which I don't," said Dominique. "Ben and I had to sit talking to him for, like, half an hour while he told me about his dad's landscaping business. *And* he spilled his drink on my cell. I'm totally unfriending him on Facebook."

"What about Ben?" asked Lindsay. "Did anything happen at all?"

"He'd probably have been all over me if Spencer hadn't gotten in the way—I mean, I *did* catch him checking me out while we were sitting there, before he ended up leaving me alone with Spencer for the rest of the night. I think it's one of those things where he wants to be a good guy and let Spencer have a chance with me first. So all I have to do now is make sure Ben knows I'm interested in *him* and not his friend— then he'll be all mine."

"But wait," said Lindsay, "Ben never came back to the party."

"He said he was tired and that he was going to his room to sleep."

"So he totally just crawled into bed at eleven at night in the middle of a party that *he* was throwing? Isn't that, I don't know, a little psycho or something? I mean, yes, he's überhot and smart, and his party *was* pretty awesome, but—"

Emily peeked over her shoulder to get a look at Dominique's

face, trying to see if she was truly hurt over Ben ditching her at the party or if she just saw him as another boy-toy plaything. It was right then that Emily spotted *him*.

Nick Brown walked into the cafeteria, a bulky camera in hand, and began to take photos of random people eating. He was taller than she remembered. Maybe he'd grown over the summer. Worst of all was that he looked almost cute: The gash on his face had healed, leaving only the slightest hint of a scar. Yet another injustice: The boy responsible for her sister's death was left with barely a mark himself.

"…I guess Ben's got 'issues' or something…."

Despite his new height, Nick probably weighed the same now as he had then. He'd become painfully skinny, almost skeletal. His black T-shirt hung loose against his arms and chest, and his skinny hipster jeans looked like they were made for some too-thin fashion model. His arms strained against his massive camera, a huge Nikon with a telephoto lens and a thick strap that ran around his neck.

"…would still totally let him take me to homecoming…"

Nick approached a group of students, who looked up at him, confused.

"Yearbook candids," he said, and the tableful of people all swarmed to be in front of the camera, some smiling, others making stupid faces or *V*s with their fingers. *Click.* The flash went off, and Nick walked over to another group.

Emily turned away so that he wouldn't see her face as he got closer. She sat frozen in place. It was too late now. He'd see her if she stood. How could she have been so stupid, sitting here in the middle of the cafeteria just so she could listen in on some dumb story about a party?

Would Sara have sat here at lunch like this, listening to gossip? Of course not. Sara was the Machine. She would have been in the weight room working on her leg strength or hunched over her homework, getting an early start so she'd have more time to sleep later. And now Sara couldn't do any of those things. Because of him.

"Yearbook," said Nick as he arrived at Dominique and Lindsay's table. Emily didn't dare look over at them, but she could imagine them leaning up against each other, smiling evilly. The camera clicked, and the flash caught the corner of Emily's eye. She heard footsteps. Someone was approaching her from behind.

"Yearbook," he said. Emily didn't turn. She felt him standing behind her. There would be no escape now. The hairs on her arms rose, and her heart began to beat double time. The light from the windows pulsed in and out with each rapid breath she took. She sat paralyzed.

"Yearbook," he repeated.

She turned her head ever so slightly so that she could look at him out of the corner of her eye. When he saw her profile, the blood seemed to drain out of Nick's face.

"—Sara?"

Emily steeled her jaw, grabbed her backpack, and walked away as fast as she could, leaving her food on the table. Hearing her sister's name in itself was enough to make her want to cry—but hearing it from *him*? She felt his eyes burning through her back as she walked. All she wanted was to make it to the girls' room before she started crying.

By the time school ended, Emily was mostly recovered from the drama earlier that day. Still, she was in no mood to endure further stress, and she rushed to the locker room as she usually did, hoping to beat the other girls there and change before they arrived.

Throughout her elementary school swim practices, Emily had seen nothing odd about stripping naked around her teammates. She'd viewed her body as a vehicle built for motion: the twin engines of her arms and legs, the drag-resistant slope of her shoulders.

Then in seventh grade she'd sprouted breasts, and everything had changed. Suddenly, the machine of her body carried two useless lumps, slowing her times and getting in the way of her arms—and she'd become instantly shy about stripping down in front of the other girls.

She'd started changing in bathroom stalls until Dominique caught on and began speculating that she was hiding something: *I'm not saying anything, but don't you think Emily kind of looks like a guy?* Finally, Emily forced herself back into the locker room, and although the rumors of a secret Y chromosome subsided, a new set of insults emerged.

Dominique always seemed to notice Emily's "deformities" first. She'd glance over at Emily as she was changing and deliver her observations as either backhanded compliments or annoying questions.

"It's awesome that your hips are so small. That probably decreases your drag through the water."

"You're lucky your feet are so huge. They're almost like flippers or something. Like a duck."

"Do you think having one breast slightly bigger than the other makes you curve to the right as you swim? How do you adjust for that?"

And thus began Emily's new swimsuit-changing system. To avoid Dominique and the other girls, she would always arrive at practice first and leave last. Her dad called it dedication to the sport; Emily called it self-preservation.

As soon as she got to the locker room, Emily pulled out her suit and changed. Once the nylon fabric covered her, she felt an immediate sense of relief. There'd be no new insult from Dominique today. As Emily gathered her hair beneath her rubber swim cap, she heard other swimmers approaching, their laughter echoing off the locker room's tiled walls.

"I heard she was crying at lunch today," said Dominique as the door creaked open. "Paula totally heard her sobbing in a bathroom stall."

"Over a boy, you think?" asked Lindsay.

Over Sara, thought Emily. *Would they still talk like that if they knew what I was really crying about? Probably.*

"As if a boy would even touch her," said Dominique. "Emily—she's basically not a person. Dating her would be like dating a toaster. She's a robot. A swimbot. Oh! Swimbot. I think *someone* just got a new nickname!"

The girls appeared from behind a row of lockers and ceased their conversation as they noticed Emily. An awkward silence settled in the room.

"Hello," said Emily with a half smile, hoping to pretend she'd heard nothing. Dominique, though, had other plans.

"Hel-lo," mocked Dominique in a robot voice. "I. Am. Swimbot." She moved her arms in jerky motions, like Emily had seen b-boys do on *America's Best Dance Crew.* "Hel-lo. Hu-man."

Lindsay was in hysterics, hiding her smile behind a hand and crying with laughter.

"Take me. To. Your. Leader," continued Dominique.

"That's an alien," corrected Emily. "Not a robot."

"Alien. Does. Not. Compute."

More girls had arrived and were peeking around the corner, laughing at Dominique's impression.

"Just stop it, okay?" said Emily.

"Stop. What?" asked Dominique. "Need. Fuel. Give me. Weird. Almond. Butter. Flax. Seed."

Just hold it together, thought Emily. *Don't let her see how it gets to you.* Keeping her cool would have been hard enough under normal circumstances. But today? After seeing Nick Brown in the cafeteria? After hearing him call her Sara?

"Nobody. Asks me. Out," Dominique continued. "Why don't. Human boys. Like me?"

The growing crowd of girls laughed even harder, and Emily felt her face go red.

"I haven't seen you with a whole lot of boyfriends, either,

Dom," said a voice from behind Emily. "I think I'm starting to see why."

Emily turned around to see Samantha Hill, the captain of the girls' varsity team, staring down at Dominique. Although only five foot seven, Samantha had a presence that made her seem six feet tall. It didn't hurt that she was model-gorgeous without a speck of makeup. She had supposedly thrown last year's prom king out of a speeding car when he tried to touch her leg on the way home from the dance. She definitely wasn't above hitting a girl.

The locker room went silent as Samantha leaped to the top of a wooden bench.

"Listen up, ladies. Save your insults for those girls from Wilson or Jackson High. Dominique, you two are teammates. You're worried Emily might be better in the pool? Work harder. You think you're so hot that you want to offer Emily some dating advice? Get your own boyfriend first. And don't flatter yourself. I've seen you getting out of the water and without that mountain of concealer, you look like a before model in an acne-cream ad."

Samantha hopped down from the bench, opened a locker, and took out her suit. The crowd of girls was still staring at her, too shocked to speak. Samantha turned back and, noticing they were still there, barked, "We're done here. Go. Now." The girls scattered like flies off a kicked Dumpster.

"Thanks," Emily said when the other girls had scurried to their lockers. She turned away quickly, trying to avoid staring directly at Samantha as she pulled off her clothes.

"Don't think I'm your friend," said Samantha, glancing at her. Then, after a second, she added, "You know, you remind me of your sister. I mean, you look just like her." There was something odd about the way Samantha said it, though, as if she'd known Sara pretty well. As far as Emily knew, Sara had barely talked to the other kids at school. She'd certainly never brought any friends home, or even mentioned anyone by name.

"Yeah, we used to get that a lot," said Emily. She paused before asking, "Were you and Sara—friends?"

"I wouldn't say that," said Samantha, pulling on her suit. "We—never mind." Her eyes moved back and forth, as if she were thinking intently about something. Finally, she closed her locker door and tucked her hair under a swim cap. "What a hassle," she muttered, shoving loose black strands under the rubber. "You ever just think of shaving it all off?"

"Not really," said Emily, wondering why Samantha had changed the subject so suddenly. She tried to imagine the beautiful girl in front of her with a shaved head.

"Hair," said Samantha, pulling her swim cap on tight, "is overrated."

As an elementary-schooler, Emily had gone on a class trip to Oregon and watched the salmon swimming upstream. The fish beat their tails fast against the current, leaped from the water, and then dove back in, defying the river to push them to the ocean.

"Mrs. Turner," she remembered saying, "they're doing the breaststroke."

Since then, Emily had imagined herself as a salmon when she did the breaststroke, reaching her arms forward and yanking her torso out of the water. The stroke was the sport's messiest and most violent—requiring the swimmer to assault the water's surface.

Today, Emily attacked the pool with particular fury, pretending it was Dominique's stupid robot face. But as she completed a few laps, she realized it was something else that had truly upset her. Emily's conversation with Samantha replayed in her head:

"Were you and Sara—friends?"

"I wouldn't say that."

Sara had never mentioned any enemies, but she must have had them. Any great swimmer did. Yet something in Samantha's tone had indicated more than an in-the-pool rivalry. But what else could it have been? As far as she knew, there *was* no Sara outside of the pool. She was the Machine, built to crush records and nothing more.

When Emily reached the far end of the lane, she realized she'd been swimming at full speed, blowing past the girls in the other lanes. As she grabbed the side of the pool, she sucked air, and her arms began to ache.

Great, she thought. *And I've still got two hours of practice to go.*

As Emily's breathing evened out, she looked up to see her father silhouetted against the sharp overhead lights. His impressive gut cast a large shadow over her.

"Kessler!" he said. "What do you think you're doing?"

Kessler? she thought. *Really?*

"Just taking a little break—*Coach*."

A few of the other girls were treading water, watching this little exchange.

"And who around here said you could do that?" Coach Kessler looked slowly and deliberately over each of his shoulders as if checking for phantom assistants. "You stop when I tell you to stop."

"But, Dad—"

"Coach."

"Fine. Whatever."

He crouched down and brought his face a few inches from hers.

"You just bought yourself another hour in the pool—"

"But—"

"You want to go for two?"

Emily shook her head.

"No, sir." *Looks like being the coach's daughter won't get me any special treatment*, she thought. *Kind of the opposite.*

"That's better," he said. He turned and walked a few lanes over, deliberately ignoring her to check in on a few of the weaker swimmers. As Emily turned and positioned herself against the side of the pool to push off for a round of backstroke, Dominique's head surfaced in the next lane.

"Making trouble already, eh, Swimbot?"

Emily's heart was still beating hard from her sprint a

minute earlier. She ignored Dominique and concentrated on her form: feet pressed against the wall shoulder-width apart, her legs tensed, ready to push off.

"Backstroke's not your race," said Dominique. "You might just want to, you know, forget about it. Concentrate on some strokes where you actually stand a chance of winning."

Dominique arranged her body against the side of the pool as Emily had, and the girls turned their heads to look at each other. Emily was still breathing hard, and Dominique smiled, recognizing her weakness.

"I'm trying to remember—have you *ever* beaten me at backstroke?"

"You haven't seen me swim it in competition since May," said Emily, her knuckles going white around the lip of the pool. The block, which would have been far easier to grip, stood at the far end of the lane.

"Then I guess you wouldn't mind a little race?" said Dominique. "There and back?"

"Not at all."

Stupid, thought Emily, still trying to catch her breath. *She can tell I overextended myself. She's trying to make me look bad.* Indeed, most of the other swimmers were watching Emily and Dominique talk. Some were treading water and whispering to one another.

"Three," said Dominique, tensing her legs. "Two. One."

The girls pushed off in unison, streaking for a few meters beneath the water before rising side by side and beginning their strokes. They glided on the pool's surface like weightless insects, matching each other move for move. As they cut down the lanes, Emily looked at the overhead flags, readying herself for the turn at the far wall.

And then she heard them chanting; the other girls on the team were cheering, "Dominique! Dominique!"

How could they all be cheering against me? Emily wondered.

Because you're a machine, a voice inside her responded. *Just like your sister.* She suddenly thought of the story of John Henry, hammering his way through the mountain, racing against the locomotive.

Everyone wants to see the human win, she realized. *No one cheers for the machine.*

The revelation hit her at the same moment the back wall collided with her skull. Pain radiated from her bruised head, coming down through her body in waves. Even worse than the physical anguish, though, was the shame. Emily couldn't believe it: She'd gotten distracted and lost track of the flags, something she hadn't done since elementary school.

There was no point in finishing. Emily surfaced and looked down the lane as her rival completed the race. A few seconds later, Dominique touched the far wall to a loud cheer from their teammates, and several swam over to her to offer their congratulations.

Emily stood alone at her end of the pool, her stomach knotted with humiliation.

It's just practice, she tried to remind herself. *You'll have all year to beat her.* But it was little consolation. The room echoed with light applause as Dominique, surrounded by her admirers, threw a fist in the air. The other girls would remember this moment: Swimbot breaking down, losing a race to a mere human.

At dinner that night, Emily's mother tried desperately to make conversation as Emily and her father glowered at each other from opposite sides of the table.

"So, how was work?" she asked Emily's dad.

"Fine," he responded. "Except that *one* of the swimmers had a discipline problem and then tried to show off by having a little race—which she *lost*, by the way."

"Well, what about you, Emily?" her mom asked hopefully.

"Fantastic. Except the stupid *coach* made me practice for an extra hour for basically no reason."

Emily's mom nervously knotted her napkin in her hands. She avoided eye contact with her husband and Emily and looked across the table at the empty spot where Sara used to sit.

"Well," she said, trying to maintain her smile, "it sounds like everyone could use a little cheering up, and I have just the thing. A pint of a certain pair of people's favorite ice cream that may or may not contain delicious dark chocolate fish—"

Emily's mouth immediately started watering. She hadn't been allowed to have ice cream since her birthday in August, and the only chocolate she'd tasted since then came in the form of chalky protein shakes that reminded her more of liquid cardboard than cocoa beans.

"Not for her," said Emily's father. "She's already had her eight thousand calories, and that much sugar and fat would be terrible for her system, especially this soon before bedtime."

Emily's mother frowned.

"Well, just a few scoops couldn't possibly hurt—"

"I said no."

Emily popped a pair of vitamins from the side of her plate and finished the last of her water.

"It's fine, Mom," she said. "He's right. I'm not hungry anyway."

A few hours later, after Emily had plowed through a mountain of homework, including forty pages of reading for Honors History, she sat on her bedroom floor, stretching her aching muscles. After a week of intense training and equally intense homework, Emily wasn't sure which hurt worse, her body or her head. She heard a soft knock on the door and opened it to find her mom holding a coffee mug.

"I brought you some 'tea,'" she said with a wink, handing the mug to Emily, who took it in both hands. The ceramic was cold to the touch, and Emily looked down to see not tea but ice cream.

"I figured a few hundred calories couldn't hurt," Emily's mom said. "Besides, conditioning is an art, not a science. Even your father says that."

Emily looked down at the ice cream, wanting it more than anything. She pressed the top of a scoop with her index finger and brought it to her lips. The entire focus of her being suddenly centered at the tip of her tongue and the sensation of chocolaty sweetness.

She took a deep breath and handed the mug back to her mother.

"Mom—I can't."

"But—"

"Sara wouldn't have eaten a mug of ice cream," said Emily, and her mother looked away.

"Right," she said. "Of course." She hesitated for a moment, watching the melting ice cream, as if hoping Emily would change her mind. After a few seconds had passed and Emily stayed silent, her mother said good night.

She turned down the hall, dipping a spoon into the mug and eating as she went. Emily closed the door behind her. She felt bad for her mom—she was always trying stuff like that. She'd been the one who insisted Sara and Emily go to public school instead of the private swim academy their father had wanted them to attend. In the end, they'd compromised on Twin Branches High, which had a good pool and was located close to Las Playas, where Junior Nationals was held each year.

What Emily's mom didn't seem to realize was that deep down Emily and Sara *wanted* to follow their dad's strict regimen. If anything, their desire to win was even stronger than his. Or at least that's what Emily told herself. She had to admit, that ice cream had tasted even better than she remembered.

Later that night, Emily checked her phone and texted Kimi to see if she was up. When no response came, she opened her laptop and decided to check her G-Chat. The cell and the computer, Emily's two most prized possessions, were hers thanks to her mom.

Although Emily's dad had initially resisted them as "unnecessary gadgets" that would only serve as temptations to talk to strange boys, Emily's parents had eventually struck a bargain: As long as Emily kept her GPA above 3.5 and stuck to her training regimen, she was allowed to have the phone and the laptop—as well as a monthly sleepover with Kimi.

As Emily signed on to her IM account, she thought back over the events of the day. After the locker-room encounter with Dominique and Samantha and that stupid race, she'd almost forgotten her earlier run-in with Nick Brown.

She flashed back to the astonished look on his face and the way he'd called her Sara. She winced as if in physical pain every time the incident played in her head.

As she waited for her log-in to complete, Emily tried to think of something pleasant, and Ben immediately came to mind. She remembered Dominique's story about the party, about the way he'd totally ditched her and headed back to his room to sleep. Other guys were powerless against Dominique's supposed charms, but not him. She wondered what he'd thought of as he went to bed that night. For a moment, Emily let herself fantasize that it was her.

She absently checked her in-box (nothing but junk mail) and her Facebook feed (no new invites, posts of interest, hookups, or breakups). According to the site, she had thirty friends. In real life, all she had was Kimi, who she hoped was still online.

> *EmilyK14:* Kimi? You there?
>
> *ChEnigma22:* Hey! Sorry I missed u at lunch! Was totally hiding out from Amir Singh!
>
> *EmilyK14:* Who?
>
> *ChEnigma22:* Ugh. You remember him from when he tried to recruit us for his hypernerdy role-playing game, right? TOTAL stalker. Wants to be my homecoming date. NOT gonna happen. I've got a list of like ten other guys who I want to ask me tho. I'm doing pro/con spreadsheets for all of them. ☺
>
> *EmilyK14:* ?
>
> *ChEnigma22:* I'll e-mail the one for Phil Ramirez. He's my top choice.
>
> *ChEnigma22:* Sending . . . NOW!

Candidate: Phil Ramirez	
Pros	**Cons**
HOT (10/10!).	Possible Axe Bodyspray user.
Plays guitar (electric!).	2.32 GPA (might lower future $ potential).
Owns/drives Mustang convertible.	Crazy exes (at least three!).
DJ skills. Plays at lots of parties.	Soul patch (could be shaved).
Six-pack abs. Sexy.	Uses the term "bro."
Senior = prom potential.	Senior = gone next year.

The list went on for several more rows. Some of the cells were highlighted in different colors, which seemed to indicate Kimi had developed a scoring system for weighting each quality, but it was way too complicated for Emily to understand.

EmilyK14: Sounds like a winner.
ChEnigma22: Yeah…Except I heard a rumor that he's already dating Paula de Veer. And he's never even said hi to me.
EmilyK14: Aw. YOU just gotta say hi.
ChEnigma22: When? He's always with his posse of dudes at school. I need to catch him when he's DJing. Like at a

party. Too bad we NEVER GET
INVITED.

ChEnigma22: Not that you care, I guess…

Emily thought of Ben Kale at one of his parties, bored,
looking for someone to talk to.

EmilyK14: Actually I sort of wish we could go
to a party, too. Not that my dad would
let me.
ChEnigma22: !!!
ChEnigma22: There's hope for you yet! We're
GONNA make this happen!
ChEnigma22: Er. Eventually.
ChEnigma22: Like by the time we're seniors.
☹
EmilyK14: ☹
ChEnigma22: Aw! G2G. But sorry again
about missing u at lunch. Any adven-
tures w/o me?

Emily stared at the screen for a moment, her fingers hovering over the keys.

ChEnigma22: U there?
EmilyK14: Nah. Nothing major.
ChEnigma22: K. Sleep tite! See u tomorrow!
EmilyK14: Nite.

Emily logged off, closed her laptop, and flopped onto her bed. She felt bad for holding back, but the story of today's swim practice was just too embarrassing to talk about.

More than that, she'd wanted to tell Kimi what had happened with Nick, but when the time had come, she just couldn't type the words. *Hey, you know that guy who was driving the night Sara died? Well, I totally bumped into him today in the cafeteria!* Ugh. What a bunch of stupid drama. Why couldn't Nick Brown have left her alone? They just had to make it through *one* year, and then he'd be gone.

Emily pulled off her jeans and T-shirt and slipped under the covers. No matter how long she showered after practice or how much shampoo she used, her hair still smelled of chlorine afterward. Her pillow reeked of it. But Emily had gotten used to the smell; it was her sister's and her own.

In the dark of her bedroom, with the covers pulled tight around her, she could almost imagine everything was fine. She tried to concentrate on things that made her happy: the trophies lining her wall, the feeling of water on her skin, and Ben Kale.

CHAPTER
FOUR

The next time Emily saw Ben was right before swim practice.
School had just ended for the day, and most of the other kids
had already left. Emily was at the intersection of the school's
three main hallways and the long corridor leading to the
indoor pool when she saw two figures approaching fast. One
was medium-sized, the other huge: Ben and Spencer. She
could just barely make out what they were saying as they ran
toward her.

"Mission accomplished," said Spencer as they neared
Emily. "Dominique is going to freak. I totally owe you one."

"Are you kidding?" asked Ben. "This is the most fun I've
had all year."

As they reached the intersection, Spencer pointed down a
hallway to his right.

"Better split up," he said. "Rendezvous at your place in thirty?"

"I'll see you there." Looking around, Ben noticed Emily for the first time. Pausing to catch his breath, he said, "Hey, it's you. Yogurt."

Emily frowned. This wasn't how she'd imagined their next conversation going.

"My name isn't Yogurt."

"Sure," he said. "Look. Do me a favor. If school security comes by, tell them I ran that way, okay?" He pointed down a random hallway before turning toward the door to the girls' bathroom. "Oh—there's no one in there, right?"

"I don't—" But before Emily could say another word, Ben had slipped inside. She stood stupidly for a moment, waiting to hear shrieks from inside. Everything was quiet. Lucky guy.

She hesitated. Practice would be starting soon, and her dad didn't appreciate tardiness, to say the least. But if she waited here long enough, Ben would come out of the bathroom and talk to her. Maybe he'd even learn her name.

As she waited, a man in a brown school-security uniform ran up. He looked down at her menacingly through dark sunglasses. The name tag on his chest read OFFICER MONTE.

"Hey, you," he said. "See anyone run by?"

He scratched a bead of sweat from his black mustache and rubbed it against his pant leg. His nose twitched as if he were a bloodhound, tracking Ben and Spencer by scent.

"Uh—" said Emily.

"A correct response would be either yes or no," the officer

said. He looked suspiciously over Emily's shoulder at the bathroom door.

"A couple of guys ran off that way," said Emily, pointing down the hall that Ben had indicated earlier. Without another word, Monte ran down the hallway at full speed, one hand on his hat to keep it from blowing off.

"He gone?" asked Ben from inside the girls' room.

"Yeah."

Ben opened the door and peeked out.

"Wow," he said. "Girls write *way* dirtier stuff on the bathroom walls than guys do. I didn't see you mentioned anywhere, though. Too bad."

"Well, most people don't call me Yogurt."

"I know. But Emily Kessler? That's just so, I don't know—boring. Yogurt suits you way better."

For a moment, Emily was speechless. He knew her name. He must have asked someone about her. Maybe he'd even Googled her—or Facebook-stalked her! Her photos didn't show up to strangers, right? Kimi had posted that one of them dressed up like Uma Thurman and Lucy Liu in *Kill Bill* for Halloween!

"Uh, Yogurt?"

"That's not my name!" Emily said, crossing her arms, but she couldn't keep from smiling. There was no doubt about it. He was flirting with her.

"Hey!" They heard a shout at the end of the hall. "You! Stop right there!"

"That would be my cue to leave," said Ben as they looked

down the hall to see Monte charging toward them full-speed. "Maybe I'll see you again sometime."

"Maybe," she said. "Anyway, I'd better get to practice."

He was backing up now, ready to turn and run.

"You never know when swim practice might be canceled!" he shouted. "I'll see you around!"

Ben turned and fled, Officer Monte following close behind. For a moment, Emily stood watching them, trying to make sense of what had just happened. Ben Kale knew her name, had just spent two minutes flirting with her, and had said he wanted to "see you again sometime." But what did he mean about practice being canceled? She walked down the empty hall toward the pool.

The rest of the swim team, still in their street clothes, stood by the blocks as Emily entered the gym. The girls peered nervously at the water as Emily's dad paced back and forth, swearing under his breath. The pool was green. Bright green. And instead of chlorine, it smelled like apples.

"Uh, what's going on?" Emily whispered to Hannah Carmichael as she joined the crowd.

"Apparently some *boys* dumped, like, thirty vials of green food coloring into the pool. And maybe some other stuff, too, based on the smell."

"I think it smells kinda yummy," said Amanda, a cute, red-haired girl who was one of the weaker swimmers on varsity and a notorious airhead. "I kind of want to drink it."

"No one's drinking it!" shouted Emily's dad. "No one's so

much as dipping a pinkie toe in there until we drain the thing and pump in fresh water. Who knows what chemicals are in there? I'm not getting sued by some mother whose daughter's skin turns green."

"So is practice canceled?" asked Lindsay hopefully.

"Absolutely not," said Emily's dad. "The school still has a weight room, doesn't it? Unless someone turned that green, too."

So much for Ben's plan of getting practice canceled. The girls muttered insults and cursed their luck as they marched toward the locker room to change into workout clothes. Lindsay and Amanda breathed in deeply as they left the room, filling their nostrils with the pleasant apple scent.

"You two, wait," said Emily's dad, pointing to Emily and Dominique. "I'm pulling you out for the first hour to talk to a reporter, Maria St. Claire from *Swimmer's Monthly*. I believe I mentioned she'd be coming? She's waiting in the hall."

The two girls exchanged a worried glance. This sounded like a bad idea.

"She's talking to us together?" asked Emily.

"Is there a problem with that?"

Yes, Emily thought. *There's a big problem: Dominique and I hate each other!*

She smiled weakly.

"No problem at all, Coach."

Five minutes later, Maria St. Claire had shaken the girls' hands, introduced herself, and escorted them into an empty

56

classroom, where she pulled three combination desk-and-chair sets together to form a group.

Up close, the overpowering citrus scent of the reporter's perfume made Emily's eyes water. There was something too neat about the woman that set Emily on edge. Miss St. Claire's mascara seemed so carefully applied that Emily wondered if she'd done it one lash at a time, and her eyebrows were heavily plucked and redrawn in dark makeup, as if she'd gotten overzealous with a pair of tweezers and had to make up for it later.

Miss St. Claire whipped out her laptop and began to tap furiously at her keyboard as she asked them questions. The first few were pretty standard: *How much time do you spend practicing? How's your life different from a typical high school student's? What gives you a leg up on all the other young swimmers out there?*

Emily smiled and gave the same polite answers she'd rehearsed in her head. *I practice every day. I'm just a normal high school kid. As far as winning goes, I just want it more.*

"Okay," said Miss St. Claire. "Now for the juicy stuff. As two of the top swimmers in your age group in the nation, do you ever find the rivalry spilling from the pool into the outside world?"

Dominique and Emily looked at each other nervously. Uh-oh. This story was no puff piece: Miss St. Claire was here to get some dirt. Emily imagined the headline now: POTENTIAL OLYMPIANS IN THE WATER, SPOILED BRATS ON DRY LAND.

"Outside the pool—" started Emily.

"We're totally friends," said Dominique. "I mean, not BFFs or anything, but we're definitely—close."

"Is that right?" asked Miss St. Claire, looking doubtful. "Several people I talked to seemed to think that—"

"I think it's hard," interrupted Dominique. "Er, for other people to understand the kind of competitive spirit that gets into you when you swim at the highest level. But if it comes off as anything but an in-the-pool rivalry, that's just—wrong."

Looking disappointed, Miss St. Claire hit the Delete key several times and scrolled down her list of notes, searching for a new line of questioning. As she got to something near the bottom, she looked at Emily and smiled.

"Dominique," she said. "Thanks so much for your time. If you don't mind, I've got a few more questions for your 'friend.'"

Dominique got up, a strange mix of emotions on her face. *She's glad to be done with the interview*, thought Emily, *but worried about what I'll say once she's gone.*

"Not a problem," Dominique said. "Thanks *so* much for the questions." She glared at Emily with a look that said *Don't screw this up.* "See you later, Em." She left the room, her blond ponytail swishing behind her.

As Dominique closed the door, Miss St. Claire turned back to Emily. Her eyes sparkled with something, but was it genuine concern or false sincerity?

"Emily, it's clear to me that you're the real story here."

"Huh?"

"I'm talking about your motivations. Yes, clearly you and Dominique both want to win—but with you it goes deeper."

What was Miss St. Claire getting at? Emily's parents had tried to make her visit a counselor after Sara's death to talk through her grieving, but she'd hated it and refused to speak during her sessions, and after a couple of unproductive months, they'd given up. She felt like she was back in that therapist's office now.

"I have no idea what you're talking about," she said.

"Fine," said Miss St. Claire. "I should be more direct. Emily, you come from a family of successful swimmers…"

She trailed off, as if hoping Emily would get the hint. Emily ignored her and looked out the window, where the sun hung low in the sky.

Miss St. Claire continued. "Your father, Coach Kessler, is of course a former Olympian"—Emily refused to react—"and your sister, Sara, set a Juniors Nationals record at the age of sixteen, before her tragic death last spring. What's it like trying to live up to such a legacy?"

Emily felt like she'd been punched in the gut. She tried to speak, but nothing came out.

"Emily?" asked Miss St. Claire.

Emily sat perfectly still, acting as if Miss St. Claire was some horrible dinosaur that could see its prey only when it moved. No such luck.

"Emily, help me out here. How does it feel to have that kind of fam—"

"How do you think it feels?"

"Well, I don't know, sweetie. That's why I'm asking you."

Emily's face was getting hot with blood.

"It's just—it's just so stupid. I could sit here and explain how I can't get into a pool without thinking of my older sister, or how I follow the *exact* same training regimen my dad designed for her, even her sleep schedule down to the minute. Or how before I ever check my times against Dominique's, I check them against Sara's."

Miss St. Claire was typing furiously, trying to get every word.

"Sara—" said Emily. "She could have won medals, too. Way more than my dad ever did. But she didn't get to. And if I don't work just as hard as she would have—if I don't live up to that—I mean, what was it all for? And now here you are asking all these questions about her, just trying to turn all this into some kind of—some kind of *story*."

"You've got me all wrong," said Miss St. Claire, stopping her typing for a moment to look Emily in the eye. "Of course I'm looking for the best story, but I'm on your side. I'm going to make you a hero. I'm going to make you a star."

The *Swimmer's Monthly* article came out three weeks later. Emily's father flopped it down in front of her as she ate a bowl full of hard-boiled eggs, and she nearly choked on one when she saw the cover. It was her, tearing through the water, a wet spray hanging in the water beside her outstretched arms. The headline read: AMERICA'S BEST SHOT FOR GOLD: HOW ONE GIRL'S QUEST TO FULFILL HER SISTER'S LEGACY FUELS AN OLYMPIC DREAM.

"Congratulations," said Emily's father, beaming. "You're famous."

Emily felt sick.

"Dad," she said, "the cover? Really? Now everyone in school is going to think I'm—that I'm—"

"A great swimmer," he said. "And I don't think too many kids at the high school read *Swimmer's Monthly*."

And he might have been right—

Except that the next Friday, both the school paper and the local one picked up the story and ran it on the front page.

And the next day, a local TV station requested an interview.

And the next morning, a reporter for *Sports Illustrated* called.

"This is awesome," said Kimi as she flipped through *Swimmer's Monthly* on Emily's bed that Sunday. "She makes you sound like a frickin' superhero, or a rock star, or LeBron James or something. And the best thing is Dominique! All she gets are, like, two lines in the final paragraph!"

Emily winced. "Great. So now Dominique is going to totally hate me."

"Aw, don't be so upset. She already hated you."

"Why couldn't that stupid reporter have just left me

alone?" asked Emily as she reread the story on the *Swimmer's Monthly* website. "I haven't even won anything, not really. This is just too much—attention."

Kimi sat up and laid down the magazine. "You're joking, right? This is the best thing that's ever happened to us. You're going to be totally famous now. Forget sitting in the corner of the cafeteria. Forget boys completely ignoring us. Forget never getting invited to parties. We're in!"

"Not to burst your bubble or anything," said Emily, "but it's just a stupid story. No one at school reads the newspaper. No one cares."

Kimi flopped onto her stomach and groaned into one of Emily's pillows, then turned her head to look at Emily, a pleading expression on her face. Emily closed the *Swimmer's Monthly* website and opened a fresh window.

"Em, don't do this. You always do this! Something good happens and you find a way to—"

"Kimi—"

"No! Don't interrupt. What I'm saying is, you always find a way to take some awesome thing that just happened and make it look like a complete—"

"Kimi!"

"What?"

Emily carried her laptop over to the bed and turned the screen toward Kimi.

"I just logged onto Facebook."

"Yeah. And?"

"And I have one hundred and sixty new friend requests."

CHAPTER FIVE

The next day in homeroom, as the other students caught up on homework or sleep, Alicia walked over to Emily's desk and laid down a copy of the school paper.

"I didn't realize I was in the presence of greatness—or at least future greatness. Now, why, exactly, have you been hiding this from everyone?"

Emily shrugged. "I wasn't hiding anything."

"You're not like most kids your age, you know," said Alicia. "When I was a freshman, which wasn't all that long ago, I would have given anything to be a celebrity—but mostly just because I wanted to date Justin Timberlake."

"He's a little old for me," said Emily. "Maybe Justin *Bieber*?"

"Just don't let it go to your head—you've got a good one

on your shoulders," said Alicia, "as this latest progress report indicates." She pulled a piece of paper out of a binder and put it on Emily's desk. "All A's so far. Including the only one at the school in Honors History. Very impressive."

"Thanks," said Emily.

"Just remember me when you're a megastar," said Alicia. "Now if you'll excuse me, I have to go kick a few butts." She patted the binder full of progress reports. "Not everyone can be an honor student."

At lunch, Kimi wouldn't let Emily sit in their usual corner spot.

"You're a celebrity now," Kimi insisted. "Act like it."

She took Emily's hand and dragged her toward the center table, each step forward filling Emily with increasing dread. She waited for the security alarms to go off and the guard dogs to attack. They were trespassing here. They didn't belong.

This was just like last summer: Kimi had persuaded her to sneak out to Red Bear Lake after the park closed for the night, and they'd had to hide in the bushes from a park ranger for almost an hour. It wouldn't have been so bad, except that the bushes turned out to be poison oak. Emily had the same feeling now, like she'd regret this intrusion for several itchy weeks to come.

The girls had been among the first to arrive at lunch, and the center table stood vacant. Emily looked down to find its surface heavily decorated in Sharpied graffiti, much of it consisting of hearts containing couples' names. Several of the hearts, though, had been filled in with black.

Breakups, thought Emily. *Ouch.*

"Okay," said Kimi, taking a deep breath. "Here goes nothing."

She put one leg over the bench.

"Kimi!" said Emily in a loud whisper. "Have you *completely* lost it? You can't just sit there. You don't have—you know—permission."

"That's not how being popular works," said Kimi, swinging the other leg over the bench. "No one gives you permission. You give it to yourself."

"Kimi—" started Emily, but it was too late. Kimi sat.

No sirens blared. No flashing lights filled the room.

"Well?" Kimi said. "Come on. Don't make me eat alone."

Emily looked around the cafeteria, checking to make sure the coast was clear. No sign of Lindsay or Dominique anywhere. She tried to imagine Ben sitting at the table, the warmth of his body right next to her.

Okay, she thought. *You can do this.*

She took a deep breath, then put her backpack down and sat next to Kimi, who was already beaming.

"Look at us," said Kimi. "Just two cool kids, sitting at the cool table, doing cool stuff. Maybe later we'll head to the mall and buy clothes at the cool-kids store, and then after that we'll go to a cool-kids party."

"Okay," said Emily, still nervous. "I get it, I get it. We're very cool."

"I knew it," said a voice from behind her. "You *have* gone completely delusional."

Emily looked over her shoulder to see Dominique settling in next to her. Dominique's blond ponytail was pulled back especially tight, giving her face the pinched look of an actress with a fresh Botox injection, and her nose was wrinkled in displeasure like a wet cat's. Dominique set down a massive tub of chicken wings before leaning over and speaking in an angry whisper. "Are you two lost or something? Your kind isn't welcome here."

"I don't know," said Kimi. She looked up at the big skylight. "I kind of like it here. It's nice and sunny. Hey—don't you think that cloud looks like a pterodactyl?"

Dominique refused to look up. She kept her eyes trained directly on Kimi's throat as if planning ways to strangle her.

"Oh, I almost forgot," said Kimi. "Did you get a chance to read that article about Emily in *Swimmer's Monthly*? I think there were even a few sentences about *you*—somewhere near the end."

Dominique pulled the top off her tub of wings, took one out, and brandished it at Emily and Kimi like a knife.

"If you think one stupid article means you're suddenly qualified to sit at *my* table, you'd better think again. You may have fooled that stupid reporter into thinking you're some kind of tragic hero, but I know exactly who you are. Swimbot, a little machine that eats and sleeps and does the butterfly stroke. And everyone else knows it, too." She brought the chicken wing to her lips, consumed it in three bites, and set the bones down on the table before continuing her rant. "So take your little sidekick and get back to that sinkhole you call a table before someone sees me sitting with you."

"Sidekick?!" asked Kimi, her face flushed. "I'll show you a 'sidekick.'" She swung her foot through the space beneath the table and just missed Dominique's knee.

"Hey!" interrupted a male voice. "You're that girl from the article, right?"

A boy with slicked-back brown hair and a polo shirt with an upturned collar settled in beside Kimi. He reeked of Axe Bodyspray.

"I'm Phil Ramirez," he said, holding out a hand. Emily took it and gave it a soft squeeze.

No way! she thought. *Phil! The guy from Kimi's spreadsheet! Not really my type, but to each her own.*

Kimi went silent. She stared at Phil and inhaled deeply. Emily almost laughed. Never once had she seen Kimi so tongue-tied.

"Nice to meet you," said Emily. "Uh, this is—"

"Kimi Single," said Kimi. "Er—I mean, Kimi Chen. But I am single. Not that it matters. Just letting you know. It's my first time sitting at the center table, and I saw a cloud shaped like a—okay, um, I'm going to shut up now."

Phil smiled and looked her in the eye.

"Nice to meet you, Kimi Single. It's good to see a couple of new faces around here. And not bad-looking ones, either," he said, half joking, half flirting.

"Unfortunately, Emily and Kimi were just leaving. Isn't that right?" asked Dominique, staring daggers at Emily.

Emily looked back at the empty table in the corner of the cafeteria where she and Kimi usually sat. From here, it looked as dark and abandoned as a city street corner at night. Next to her, she noticed Kimi stealing quick glances at Phil and trying not to stare as he waved to a few friends across the cafeteria. If she and Kimi left now, would they ever have the guts to sit here again?

"Actually," said Emily, "I kind of agree with Kimi. I *do* like it here. We'll go ahead and eat with you guys, as long as that's cool with you, Phil."

"Sure thing," he said, smiling. "It's not every day I get to eat with a future Olympian. And her cute friend."

Dominique grimaced and whispered to Emily, "You're playing a dangerous game, Swimbot. Enjoy sitting here while you can. Trust me—it won't last long." Then she leaned away, smiled, and told Phil, "I'm so glad Emily's finally sitting with us. I keep saying we need more swimmers around here!"

"I've actually been meaning to say hi," said Phil. "I knew your sister."

"Oh, huh," said Emily. "She, uh, never mentioned you."

Phil laughed. "Yeah, I bet she didn't. I was sort of a geek back then. Plus I was in my reggae phase. Not that Sara was a music snob or anything...."

As Phil spoke, Emily felt her shoulders clenching involuntarily. She hated how anything to do with Sara—even a kind word from a relative stranger—seemed to trigger an immediate flood of stress and involuntary muscle spasms.

"I only talked to her a handful of times," Phil continued, "but she seemed like a genuinely nice person. Honestly, I wish I'd known her better. Only a few people really got to. Samantha and Cam—"

"Knew who?" asked Cameron Clark as he sat between his sister and Emily. She had never seen him so up close. Like most swimmers, he smelled deeply of chlorine, and the roots of his blond hair looked wet, as if he'd recently gotten out of the pool. He seemed oddly out of place at the table; his layers of ropey muscles gave him the look of an older guy, a college student, maybe, a man among boys. Kimi couldn't stop looking at him, and even Emily had to make a conscious effort not to stare.

"Sara," said Phil. "You guys hung out all the time, right?"

"We trained together," said Cameron. "But knowing someone? That's entirely different."

"Sure," said Phil. He seemed almost scared of Cameron. "That's all I meant."

Cameron turned to Emily. "Sara was—exceptional. I hope you know that." He stared at her intensely for a moment, as if he could read her every thought with his eyes. Then he looked away.

All Emily could respond with was a muffled "Yeah."

Luckily for her, Phil seemed more socially aware than most. Reading the discomfort on Emily's face, he quickly segued to a new topic. "Uh, so has anyone heard that new mashup of Lady Gaga and Mozart? *Totally* sick." Maybe he was smarter than Kimi's spreadsheet gave him credit for.

Gradually, Emily's shoulders relaxed, and she started breathing normally. Still, as lunch continued and more people started to sit down, she wondered how many had known Sara, and throughout the rest of the meal, she noticed Cameron alternately studying her face and avoiding eye contact.

Phil stayed off the subject of Sara for the rest of lunch as he introduced Emily and Kimi to other members of the popular crowd. Many of them had heard about the article already, and the ones who hadn't were impressed by Emily's "future Olympian" credentials. A couple of guys even said they'd try to make it out to her next swim meet.

A few minutes later, Spencer showed up, and Phil introduced him to Emily. Spencer smiled and shook her hand. Without trying, he almost crushed her fingers with his grip. Up close, he was even more muscled than she'd realized before, like a high school version of the Incredible Hulk, minus the green skin.

"I know who you are," he said. "Yogurt, right?"

Emily couldn't believe it. Ben must have talked to Spencer about her.

"It's too bad Ben's not here," said Spencer. "I'm sure he'd want to invite you to his party this Friday."

"Where is he, anyway?" asked Lindsay, who had just taken a seat at the far end of the table.

"Home," said Spencer, shaking his head. "Didn't you see today's paper?"

Spencer dug into his bag and pulled out a wrinkled copy of the day's school paper. Its headline read: SCHOOL CANCELED

70

"He totally hacked the journalism class's computers last night," said Spencer, smiling proudly. "What I do to linemen out on the football field, he does to the school's firewalls. Anyway, he's suspended for the week. Normally, I think Principal McCormick would have sent him home for longer, but I guess she actually thought it was pretty funny."

"That's too bad he'll have to miss the whole week," said Emily.

"I guess you don't know Ben," said Spencer, taking out a sandwich. "His only regret is that it's such a short vacation. He was hoping he'd be gone for at least a month. Well, maybe next time."

The boys talked and joked, asking Emily about her dad's medals and what famous athletes she'd met. They were careful not to bring up her sister. *Popular guys*, she realized, *are well liked for a reason. They're unexpectedly nice. And funny. And, naturally, cute.* A warm sensation pulsed through her. *This must be how being popular feels*, she thought. She liked it.

The only one at the table who wasn't smiling was Dominique. She'd finished her massive bucket of wings unnoticed and was now staring at the pile of bones in front of her, as if wishing she could devour Emily the same way.

For the rest of the day, Emily rushed from class to class, and swim practice after school went so late that it was dark by the

time her dad drove her home. She wasn't able to decompress
and rehash the day's events with Kimi until right before bedtime, when they met online.

ChEnigma22: So—how's it feel to be
popular?

EmilyK14: ?

ChEnigma22: Don't play dumb. And Ben
Kale's BFF totally knew who you were!
I can't wait for Friday!

EmilyK14: Friday?

ChEnigma22: Uh. Hello? Ben's party. The
one Spencer invited us to?

EmilyK14: No...He said Ben would totally
invite you IF HE WAS HERE!

ChEnigma22: Don't be so literal.

EmilyK14: ...

ChEnigma22: We're going.

EmilyK14: Kimi...Even if I wanted to, my
dad would never let me.

ChEnigma22: Which is why you're not telling him.

EmilyK14: ???

ChEnigma22: On Friday night you're "going
to bed" at 10:30 like usual.

ChEnigma22: ...I'll pick you up down the
block at 10:35. ☺

EmilyK14: I'll think about it.

ChEnigma22: Em…You always say that. And
it always means no.

EmilyK14: I said I'll think about it.

At Thursday's practice, Emily set a personal record in the 200-meter freestyle. Her dad smiled as he showed her his stopwatch and made a note on his clipboard.

"See?" he said. "Our work is finally paying off."

Our work? thought Emily, catching her breath as her father waddled back to his office, which adjoined the pool, to answer his phone. Her fastest time ever—she should have been ecstatic. So why did she feel so…nothing? It was as if she had just watched somebody else swim an amazing race, like she was a ghost watching her own body cut through the water.

She remembered a story Sara had told her once, on a rare occasion when their parents had gone out and Sara was watching over her: When Alexander the Great had conquered the known world and reached the farthest sea, he'd stared out at the water and wept. According to the legend, it was because he had no battles left to fight and no enemies left to stand against him. But what if it was because of something else? What if it was because there was no one standing next to him to share his victory? Now that Emily thought about it, she realized Sara had told her that story just a few nights after she had set the record in the backstroke. Her sister had also taken Honors History.

At the other end of the pool, the girls were squealing and

looking out the huge glass window by the side of the pool. Through it, Hector Alonzo, a popular older guy, was hoisting a sign that read AMANDA, WILL YOU BE MY HOMECOMING DATE? Amanda had run up to the window, breathed hot air against the glass so that it fogged up, and coyly written YES. Maybe she was a little more clever than everyone gave her credit for.

Isn't that dance still more than a month away? Emily thought. Not that it mattered: She wouldn't be going anyway.

As Amanda skipped happily to the pool and jumped back in, the other swimmers surrounded her, offering their congratulations.

"Jealous much?" asked Dominique from the next lane over. "Or are you just planning on going to the dance with your girlfriend, Kimi?"

"Maybe I'll go with your—uh—dad," said Emily, immediately regretting the comeback as soon as it exited her lips.

"Ew," said Dominique. "But I'll let him know you're interested. I'm *sure* you two will have much more fun than me and Ben."

"You're going with Ben Kale?" asked Emily, trying to hide her sudden panic.

"Of course," said Dominique. "He just doesn't know it yet. But don't worry, after he sees what I'm wearing to his party this Friday, he'll be begging to take me to homecoming— and to do a whole lot more after the dance. I hope that's not a problem, sweetie. I kind of got the sense the other day that *you* might have a little crush on Ben, too. I hope little Swim-bot won't get her feelings hurt. Or do you even have those?"

As Dominique swam away, Emily quietly boiled with anger, so much so that she half expected the water around her to turn to steam.

Later that night, Emily texted Kimi:

Emily Kessler: Hey, so, change of plans.
Kimi Chen: ?
Emily Kessler: Tomorrow. Ben's party. I'm in.

CHAPTER SIX

For the past 812 straight days, Emily had followed her sleep schedule. Whether it was summer vacation, her birthday, Christmas, or New Year's Eve, she went to bed at ten thirty each night and woke up at six thirty the next morning, her circadian rhythms so exact that she no longer needed an alarm clock.

According to her dad, Emily's perfect sleep schedule allowed her body near-superhuman powers of recovery. As she slept, her torn muscles sewed themselves back together, stronger than before, and the weariness in her bones slowly evaporated into the night air. While her classmates and competitors might wake up groggy, Emily opened her eyes each morning as awake as if she'd just downed three pots of coffee. Not that she'd ever had coffee—her dietary regimen would never have allowed so much caffeine.

For 812 straight nights, Emily had put on the old oversize T-shirt Sara had given her for Christmas one year, downed a warm glass of milk, and fallen asleep the minute her head hit the pillow. Until tonight. Tonight, a cold Friday in October, she looked at her bedroom clock and, for the first time she could remember, read 10:31.

She tried to lift an arm and immediately felt pain in her aching biceps, sore from hours of weight lifting in the gym after school. By the last few reps, she'd barely been able to curl twenties, and involuntary spasms had flowed through her muscles as if she were holding onto an electric fence. If she got out of bed now, her muscles wouldn't have their usual rest. She'd be sore tomorrow and sleepy for the 10K morning run her dad had added to her usual schedule.

If she went to bed now, she'd keep up her 812-day streak: 813 tonight, 814 tomorrow, 815 the day after that. And on and on until she was too old to go after medals anymore. If she got out of bed, the streak would reset back down to zero.

But if she stayed in bed tonight, Dominique would be all over Ben at the party. Emily pictured Dominique showing up in a skimpy black dress, walking up to Ben, and sitting on his lap. She pictured Dominique quietly leaning over close to his ear and whispering something—

Emily threw off the covers. She was going to this party.

As quietly as she could, Emily slipped out of bed and crept slowly to her door, double-checking to make sure it was indeed locked. She jiggled the handle and felt it catch. Okay, no unexpected parental check-ins. Unless, of course, they knocked. But that would never happen, right? Her dad cared way too much about keeping her on her sleep schedule to wake her. The house could be burning down, and he'd just quietly break through the door and carry her to safety through the flames before he'd dare interrupt an REM cycle.

She took a breath. It would be okay. Just as long as she hurried and didn't make any noise as she crawled out her window. First things first, though: She needed an outfit.

Emily opened her closet and examined the jeans and T-shirt she'd selected earlier. They had seemed like a fine choice when she'd laid them out on her bed an hour ago, but now, next to the image of a party populated by pretty girls with short skirts, immaculate makeup, and magazine-perfect hair, the outfit suddenly seemed uninspired and average.

She flipped through the other clothes in her closet, mostly identical T-shirts and jeans. Emily frowned, thinking, *If a stranger looked through my clothes, she'd think I was a boy.*

Finally, as she reached the far edge of the closet, Emily's hand brushed against taffeta and lace and, as if selected by fate, the dress fell from its hanger into her arms. As she looked down at the frilly bridesmaid's dress she was holding, she remembered her cousin Kelly's wedding last summer, where she'd first worn it. All day after the ceremony, the other guests had commented on how pretty Emily was.

"You look like an actual girl," said one aunt who'd had a bit too much to drink.

Can you wear a bridesmaid's dress to a party? Emily wondered. Probably. A dress was a dress, right? And she'd looked good in it. Why would her parents have made her keep it if she wasn't supposed to wear it again? She wished that she could ask her mom what the rules were fashion-wise, but that would entail telling her mom she was going to a party. Not a chance.

She turned the dress over in the moonlight. The strapless top took attention away from Emily's broad shoulders, and the flared pink-and-white layered skirt accentuated the slight feminine curves of her otherwise boyish frame. It was the kind of dress a princess would wear to a ball in a Disney movie. And didn't those girls always get their Prince Charmings?

She gave the jeans and T-shirt one last glance, then slipped the dress over her head and opened her bedroom window. The cool night air brushed against her exposed collarbone. For the first time in a while she felt good—even, she had to admit, pretty.

"Nice—dress," said Kimi, a puzzled expression on her face. "Isn't it kind of poofy?" She pulled at the pink fabric of Emily's skirt as the two of them walked down the street and away from the house.

Emily frowned and said nothing. She quickened her pace and walked a few steps ahead of Kimi.

"Hey—forget I said anything," said Kimi. "It's not like you need fashion advice from someone who dresses like a *Realtor*, right?" Since Dominique and Lindsay had accused

Kimi of looking like a real estate agent on the first day of school, the popular girls had made sure the label stuck, never mind that Kimi hadn't worn anything remotely similar since that first day. Nonetheless, last week Kimi had arrived to find a fake Century 21 ad taped to her locker with her face Photoshopped in.

"Sorry," said Emily, feeling bad. "I didn't mean to get all passive-aggressive on you. And don't say that about yourself. You look really cute."

"I hope so," said Kimi. "Who knows what you're actually supposed to wear. But I say we *both* look hot. We're going to *own* this thing!" She adjusted her bra, which appeared to be more padded than usual, and smiled. Kimi was wearing a vintage-looking halter-top dress with polka dots, and she explained to Emily that she was going for an Asian Zooey Deschanel look.

As they got to the end of the street, the girls approached a red sports car that was blaring music into the otherwise quiet neighborhood. The car sat low on its axles and had a blazing phoenix detailed on the hood. The windows shook with each drumbeat and bass note blasting from the stereo.

"Not bad, eh?" asked Kimi. "I got Phil to drive us!"

A sudden feeling of panic filled Emily's chest. Was she really riding with Phil to Ben's party? And in *this* car?

"Uh, is something wrong?" Kimi put a hand on Emily's shoulder.

"Just—uh—I thought maybe your dad was driving us or

something," said Emily. "Or—maybe we could walk. Or ride our bikes?"

"Em—Ben's place is, like, ten miles from here. And I'm *not* getting a ride to my first high school party from my parents."

"Kimi, you know I don't like driving with—"

"I know. I know. But please, Em, just this once. Suck it up and get in. For me—and for yourself. For Ben Kale. Take a breath, get in, and close your eyes. In ten minutes, we'll be there."

Kimi opened the rear door and slid into the backseat. She gestured for Emily to come in.

Room for one more, thought Emily, recalling a ghost story about an elevator crash. She felt her breathing accelerate and wondered if she'd be the first teenager of all time to pass out *before* a party.

Just ten minutes and then you're at Ben's house. Just ten minutes. Just ten minutes.

She slid into the back of the car.

"Nice of you to join us," came Phil's voice from the front seat. Emily looked up to see him at the wheel next to his buddy Marcus Jones, who had been elected the hottest guy in school according to several anonymous polls in the girls' locker room. Marcus was six foot four, with dark skin, green eyes, and thick black hair. He was also rumored to be Denzel Washington's nephew. Emily blushed as she realized she recognized him from an underwear ad in the Sunday paper.

But as Phil turned the key in the ignition and the engine

roared to life, all thoughts of hot boys fled Emily's brain and sheer instinctual terror took over. She gripped the handle above her head, her knuckles white.

Phil turned back to look at her and smiled.

"Don't stress," he said. "I'll get you there safe." Emily willed her hand to let go, but it was no use. Phil shook his head and laughed. "Have it your way, but I'm telling you, with your arm like that, you *kind of* look like a dress on a clothes hanger."

He hit the gas pedal, sending the car rocketing forward. Emily examined the door, wondering what the car's side-impact crash-test rating was and whether it had air bags.

Nine more minutes. Nine more minutes.

The car's bass continued to blare, and Emily wished she could shut her ears like she did her eyes.

"I love this song!" shouted Phil as they sped down the road. The scenery flew by at what seemed like light speed as he merged onto the freeway, and Emily looked over his shoulder to check the speedometer.

Phil was doing sixty-five. Exactly.

Breathe, she thought. *It's okay. Seven minutes.*

"I love this song, too!" she shouted, trying to pretend that everything was fine, and Phil cranked the bass even louder.

Kimi frowned and pulled her cell out of her pocket. She scrolled down her contacts list to Phil's name and opened the "additional information" section. The list of pros and cons popped up, and Kimi added "possible future hearing loss" to the cons column.

"It's nice to meet you!" Marcus shouted back, turning his head to look at her. "I hear you went to the Olympics!"

Uh-oh. It sounded like some rumors had started to take on a life of their own.

"Maybe in 2016!" she shouted, checking the clock.

Five minutes.

"Right on!" Marcus shouted. "U.S.A.! U.S.A.!"

"U.S.A.!" shouted Kimi.

"You're a funny chick!" shouted Marcus. "When I saw you walking to the car, I thought you looked like a figure skater or something. And then Phil reminded me of that Olympics thing. Now it makes *total* sense."

Three minutes. Three… Wait. What did he mean "figure skater"?

"So—you, uh, like my outfit?" asked Emily.

"Definitely!" shouted Marcus. "It's hilarious!"

"Hilarious"? This wasn't good.

Emily had seen houses like Ben Kale's before—megamansions owned by her dad's friends from his Olympic days, paid for with money from endorsements for shoes or breakfast cereals. She just hadn't expected the party to be at a place like this.

"I'm definitely getting a house like this when I move out of my parents' place," said Phil as he parked next to a row of cars in a grassy field behind the house.

"Better get to work on that platinum record," said Marcus, smiling.

"I wish," said Phil. "This place probably costs triple-platinum money." He looked at Emily and added, "You can let go of the handle now. We're here."

Emily uncurled her hand and shook it in the air as the blood slowly returned to her fingers. The four of them got out of the car, and Phil walked around back to pop the trunk. He pulled out a large pan covered in tinfoil, lifted it to check the contents, and smiled.

"What's that?" asked Emily.

"A pony," said Phil. "What do you think it is? Ben's birthday cake. German chocolate. I baked it myself, with the help of a little lady named Betty Crocker."

"It's—it's his birthday?" asked Emily.

"Uh, yeah," said Marcus, pulling a carefully wrapped gift box out of the trunk. "Hence the birthday *party*. Now come on. Let's get in there."

As the four of them walked toward the brightly lit house, Emily looked jealously at Phil's cake and Marcus's gift.

"Great," she whispered to Kimi. "I finally start liking a guy and I don't even bring him a birthday present. Did I accidentally steal Cupid's diaper in a previous life or something so he totally hates me, or am I just really, really bad at this?"

"Do you really want me to answer that?" asked Kimi. She put an arm around Emily's waist and pulled her in for a side hug as they walked toward the massive house. "Don't sweat it. Ben obviously has plenty of *stuff* already. You just be you."

CHAPTER SEVEN

The imposing oak doors of Ben's house stood slightly ajar, and Phil pushed through them without knocking.

They opened to a large central room bookended by two curling staircases headed off in opposite directions. A hundred-piece crystal chandelier hung above a huge expanse of black-and-white-checkered tiles going for almost a hundred feet—all the way to a glass wall through which Emily saw a huge infinity pool, the kind whose edges stretch all the way to the side of a terrace, creating the appearance of water hanging in space.

There must have been a hundred and fifty people there. Emily recognized some of them from the cafeteria's center table and the few that surrounded it, but there were a few surprises: Deependu Mahajan and Eric Erickson were sitting by the pool with red cups in their hands, their jeans rolled up and their feet in the water. And Samantha Hill sat in the center of the room, leading a round of Never Have I Ever. The chandelier shone brightly off her freshly shaved head.

Emily breathed a sigh of relief: Nick Brown was nowhere to be seen.

When Phil noticed Samantha's new look, he set the cake down on a long table filled with desserts and approached her from behind.

"Now that's what I'm talking about, S-Dawg," he said. "Can I touch it?"

Samantha turned to him, her eyes blazing.

"You put a hand on me, and you'll lose it," she said. She turned back to the circle of players, and Phil took a step away. The group looked expectantly at Samantha. Emily had heard about this game but had never participated: You started by holding up ten fingers, then lowered one and sipped your drink every time you'd done the naughty thing that someone else mentioned.

"Never have I ever…kissed more than one person in a single night," Samantha said, and several guys in the group groaned and lowered their fingers. Spencer, who had just lowered his last finger, raised his red cup to the circle and downed it in a few gulps.

"We should get a drink," said Kimi.

"You mean, like, a *drink*?" asked Emily.

Spencer belched loudly and crushed the red cup in his hand.

"Maybe a root beer?" asked Kimi. "As long as it's in a red cup, no one has to know what's inside."

The girls walked over to a table filled with bottles Emily didn't recognize. Finally, she was able to track down a half-empty jug of milk. She filled a red cup.

"You're kidding, right?" asked Dominique from behind her (it seemed like she was always sneaking up on Emily). "You came to a birthday party *dressed* as a birthday cake?"

Dominique approached the table, set down her cup, and filled it with cranberry juice. When she picked up a bottle decorated with images of swans in flight and found it empty, she turned to a nearby boy, whom Emily recognized as Amir.

"Find me something to make my drink a little more *interesting*," she said. "Now."

Amir took her cup and ran to the kitchen.

Emily sipped her milk and looked Dominique up and down. She was wearing a tiny gold dress that stretched barely from her upper thighs to the top of her chest, so delicately balanced that it seemed the slightest movement would cause a wardrobe malfunction. It was the kind of dress that guys loved and girls hated—unless you were the one wearing it.

"Nice lingerie," said Kimi.

"Nice polka dots. Did you get called back in time to sell houses in the fifties?"

"I'm not a Realtor! Now why don't you head back to the Frederick's of Hollywood catalog you crawled out of and leave us alone?"

"Gladly," said Dominique. "You're not the one I wore this

for anyway. He's still hiding somewhere." Trying to find Ben, all three girls turned and looked over the sea of partiers.

"Catch you later, Swimbot," Dominique added. "You really do look great. You know, you should seriously consider accessorizing—with a scoop of ice cream."

As Dominique turned, Amir came running from the kitchen with her drink in hand. She took one sip, grimaced, and handed it back to him.

"Try again," she said as she walked toward the central room. Amir watched her go, looking down at the cup in his hands.

"Stupid," he said to himself. "Stupid."

"What are you, her butler or something?" asked Kevin, who had just walked up from behind them. Amir turned to look at him.

"I'm just being nice."

"I'm just saying, there are cooler girls at the party," said Kevin. "Don't waste your time with that one."

"I'm practicing my moves for when my ladylove, Claire, finally visits from Canada," said Amir defensively.

"Right," said Kevin. "Your long-term, megahot Canadian girlfriend who would rather spend her Friday nights playing *World of Warcraft* with you than dating the beefcake, lumberjack-looking dudes at her school."

"You doubt her authenticity?" shouted Amir, his voice's pitch growing higher. "Take it back, swine!"

"What are you two doing here?" asked Kimi, interrupting their conversation before it became too nerdy to bear.

"I always come to Ben's parties," said Kevin. "We go way back—to Odyssey of the Mind days in middle school. He practically taught me how to code."

"Speaking of which," said Amir, "I believe I spotted a certain electron-microscope prototype in his dad's office. Want to take a peek?"

Kevin turned to the girls.

"As sad as it makes me to say good-bye to you, I do actually want to go check that microscope out," he said. "Maybe I'll catch you later."

"Can you believe him?" asked Kimi, not taking her eyes off Kevin as he walked away. "Ditching girls like us to go play with some nerd toy. So lame!"

"As lame as crashing a guy's birthday party when I barely know him?" asked Emily.

"Hey! Don't you *dare* compare yourself to those geeks," said Kimi. "Who cares if you don't know him that well? Ben has totally been giving you, like, you know, signals."

As she spoke, Kimi took her BlackBerry out of her pocket, created a new file for Kevin Delucca, and in the cons column wrote *Lonely nerd*.

"You're starting a file for that guy?" asked Emily. "He doesn't seem like your usual type."

Kimi shrugged. "Most guys at school have a file. I like to be thorough."

A few minutes later, Kimi went off to find Phil, leaving Emily by herself. She was standing against a wall, looking over the sea of faces and hoping to see Ben Kale, when a voice to her left said, "There's an unexpected sight. A Kessler at a party."

Emily turned to see Cameron Clark, a drink in hand, looking down at her. She hadn't realized until now just how tall he was—six foot two at least. His tight black shirt showed off the elegant *V* of his chest, and girls all around the room kept glancing his way. Emily stared up into his cold blue eyes, speechless.

"Your sister—she wasn't the type to make it out much," he said, sipping from his cup.

"Yeah," said Emily. "Well, I'm not her."

"I know." He looked down at her, studying her face. "Sara and I used to swim together almost every morning. I guess she never mentioned me?"

Emily shook her head.

"Sara was like that," he said. "Quiet. Good at keeping secrets."

Emily was about to ask Cameron what he meant when a tall blond girl approached and stumbled into him. She wrapped an arm around his torso to steady herself, and Emily felt a sudden, unexpected wave of jealousy.

"I thought you were going to tell me about that—uh—something. Over in your car?" the blond girl said, not so subtly.

Cameron took another drink.

"Good talking to you," he said, looking over at Emily. "But as you see, I've got promises to keep."

He took the girl by the hand and led her out the front door and away from the party as Emily looked on.

Secrets, he'd said. *What did* that *mean?*

Emily looked around the party hoping to spot Kimi, and saw her close to the center of the room, standing awkwardly near the juniors and seniors, who were still playing their drinking game. Steeling up her nerve, Emily walked over and stood beside Kimi.

"Never have I ever...sucked a toe," said a Gothy girl named Dinah, and the circle said a collective "ewww" before falling silent as Spencer lowered a finger and sipped from his cup.

"Gross," said Hannah, whom Emily knew from the swim team.

"How do you even bend your feet that far?" asked Amanda. "You must be *so* flexible!"

"What?! No, I mean, it wasn't *my* toe, it was—" Spencer stopped himself from saying more. "Never mind. I took my drink. Next question."

"Looks like we have a couple of new recruits," said Samantha, patting the couch next to her and looking at Emily and Kimi. "I'm hoping you're not as innocent as you seem, or this could be a bad night for the rest of us."

The girls took a seat, even as Emily continued to scan the room for Ben. The group looked expectantly at Kimi, waiting for her to take her turn.

"Never have I ever...gone skinny dipping," she said,

looking out at the pool, and almost everyone else in the circle lowered their fingers and sipped their drinks.

"Maybe we can fix that later," said Zach Reynolds, one of the senior football players, before his girlfriend, Hannah, elbowed him in the ribs. The group turned its attention to Emily, who stared out across the room, not paying attention. Where was Ben? Had he gone to sleep early again, like at his last party? What if he—

"Em," said Kimi in a loud whisper, "your turn."

"Oh, uh, right," said Emily. "Never have I ever—"

What *had* she done? Been on a date? Made out with a guy? Gone to a dance? Held hands?

None of the above.

But probably best not to advertise any of that. She decided to avoid the topic of sex and romance altogether.

"—eaten a gummi bear."

Everyone laughed.

"What about gummi worms?" asked Spencer, and Emily shook her head. "Gummi rings? Gummi fish? Gummi dinosaurs?"

"No, no, and no."

"You poor, deprived girl."

The rest of the group lowered their fingers and sipped their drinks.

"Okay," said Spencer. "I've got one. Never have I ever kissed a guy."

"Lame," said Samantha. "That's cheating. You can't be gender specific like that."

"I didn't make the rules," said Spencer. "I just exploit the loopholes."

All the girls in the circle, Kimi included, lowered their fingers and drank. Everyone but Emily. Spencer stared at her, his mouth open.

"Seriously?" he asked. "Never?"

Emily's face turned bright red.

"You're joking, right?" asked Hannah, and Emily shook her head, ashamed.

She looked around the party. Everyone else stood in small circles, talking, drinking, and laughing—and for a moment it seemed as if the joke was at her expense. She was the only one in the circle who had never been kissed. Maybe even the only one at the party.

"That's just—sad," said Spencer.

"Leave her alone," said Samantha. "She's, like, eight years old."

"I wasn't trying to be a jerk about it," said Spencer. "I was just sur—"

"I have to go—to the restroom," Emily said, standing up.

"Em, wait," said Kimi, but Emily was already walking out of the room and up the nearby staircase, trying to get as far away from the party as possible.

"See if you can find someone to make out with on your way back!" Zach shouted before Hannah elbowed him in the ribs again.

Upstairs, Emily looked down a long hall of closed doors, trying to guess which one was a bathroom. She ran a finger under her eye and was relieved to find it dry. Good: She'd held it together pretty well so far. Still, she needed a few minutes of solitude to shake off the shame of Never Have I Ever before she faced the party again. She walked to a door in the middle of the hall and, hoping it led to a bathroom, turned the handle.

The door opened into a large, dark room. The only light came from the far wall, where a faint blue glow from a projector stretched over a large, empty space. As Emily took a step toward the light, a burst of green and yellow spread across the wall in the shape of her body, and she looked back to see a camera hooked up to a computer and pointed in her direction.

Emily jumped up and down, and the colors on the wall swirled, copying her movements. She waved her hands, and bursts of red and violet sprouted from her projection's fingertips. She couldn't help but smile. She leaned left and right, watching her image change colors and move in sync with her body. She started twirling, the poofy bottom of her dress floating around her like a parachute, and her image glowed bright white. On the wall, the edge of her skirt became a golden circle surrounding her like a ring of Saturn.

"Kind of geeky, huh?" said a voice from behind her, and Emily turned to see Ben in the doorway. Rather than the night's standard guy outfit of dark jeans and a T-shirt, he wore pajama bottoms and a Golden State Warriors jersey, as if he were ready to crawl into bed. She stopped twirling, felt her skirt settle back down around her thighs, and watched her projection fade to a cool green. Unfortunately, the room continued to spin as a wave of dizziness passed over her.

"I, uh, thought this was a bathroom," said Emily, leaning on a nightstand to steady herself. She stifled an urge to jump out the window. Couldn't she go five minutes at this party without completely embarrassing herself?

Ben smiled. "Well, I hope you figured out your mistake before you did anything regrettable in here. It wouldn't be the first time someone at one of my parties mistook this for the bathroom."

"Don't worry," said Emily. "All I did was dance like an idiot."

"Don't be too hard on yourself. You were pretty graceful, and your dress generated some really cool visuals, like it was on fire or something. Of course, I might happen to know a few tricks you don't." Ben stepped forward into the camera's field of view, and his image joined Emily's on the wall. "Watch this," he said as he raised a hand and snapped his fingers. On the wall, a shower of sparks fell from his projection's fingertips as if a firework had exploded in his hand.

Emily raised her arm into the air and unsuccessfully tried to snap her fingers. She felt her face glowing red for what had to be the thousandth time tonight—embarrassment was becoming her default setting.

She wondered if Ben had heard she'd never kissed a boy. Even if he didn't know yet, he would by the end of the night. She imagined Spencer leaning over and whispering the news in Ben's ear—and Ben trying to stifle a laugh as he realized her inexperience. Her skin glowed even redder, as if she were a strawberry Tootsie Pop or cherry Popsicle. At least it was dark in here.

She tried to snap again. Total silence. Ben looked up at her fingers, amused.

"Wait," he said. "You *do* know how to snap, right?"

She tried again, pressing her fingers together as hard as she could, but the only noise she made was the soft rubbing of skin against skin.

"I, uh, don't know how to whistle, either," she said.

"It's not too hard," said Ben. "Here, you just put your thumb against your middle finger like this—"

He took her hand and laid her fingers against each other. A few moments passed before he seemed to realize he hadn't let go, and he quickly drew his hands back as if he'd burned them on a hot stove.

"I, er, yeah, like that," he said, taking a step back and smiling a little too wide.

She tried to snap again, and a faint popping sound echoed through the room. A tiny shower of sparks appeared at her image's fingertips on the wall.

"Not bad, Kessler, not bad," said Ben.

"This is pretty cool," said Emily. "What is it? Like, a Wii or something?"

"I'm going to pretend you didn't just ask that," said Ben. "I actually designed this myself. See, the camera I set up over there sends a feed to my computer, where some software I wrote transforms the image, then sends it to that projector on that shelf."

"Huh," said Emily. "So you *do* use your brain for purposes other than hacking student newspapers and destroying swimming pools?"

"Hey, that was some of my best work," he said, smiling.

For the first time, Emily noticed a shelf full of dusty trophies at the side of Ben's room. She walked over to them and examined a certificate that read BEN KALE, 1ST PLACE, CALIFORNIA STATE TECHNOLOGY FAIR, 8TH-GRADE DIVISION.

"Those are all from a long time ago," said Ben.

"So why aren't there any new ones?" asked Emily.

"Let's just say I've seen where that path leads, and I don't want to go there."

Emily picked up another trophy and said, "I don't understand."

Ben ran a hand through his hair and stared at the floor, lost for words for the first time since Emily had met him. Finally he said, "It's like that one quote—I don't know exactly how it goes—something like, 'What's the point of gaining the world if you lose your soul?' Or, 'What's the point of success if it means you have to spend your whole life unhappy?' "

Emily blew a sheen of dust off another trophy. It read: CALIFORNIA MATH OLYMPIAD, WINNER, PRE-CALC DIVISION, 9TH-GRADE DIVISION. The dust filled her nostrils, and she coughed a few times before backing away from the trophy shelf.

"I get what you're saying," she answered, thinking over

his words carefully. "But I'm not sure it makes sense. Like, success and fun don't have to be opposites, right? And what's the *fun* in doing nothing but having fun? Wait, that doesn't quite sound right. I guess what I mean is, wouldn't you get bored after a while?"

"Constantly," said Ben, taking a step toward her. "Except for right now. For the first time in a while, I'm not bored at all."

He took another step. He was only inches from her, close enough that if he leaned forward a few more inches they'd touch.

"Emily, I—"

"Be-en! Be-en!" a voice called from down the hall. Ben's eyes went wide, and he tiptoed to the door, closing it as quietly as possible.

"Be-en!"

Emily recognized that voice. Dominique. Ben locked his door and put a finger to his lips. Footsteps approached, and a second later a loud knocking reverberated through the room.

"Ben!" shouted Dominique, slurring slightly. "I know you're in there! Let me in so we can pla-ay!"

Ben cringed as a second round of knocking began.

"She's kind of relentless, isn't she?" he whispered. "I'm not quite sure what Spencer sees in her. If he doesn't hook up with that girl soon and get her out of my hair, I'm going to have to stop inviting her to parties."

"Most guys would be flattered to have Dominique chasing after them," Emily whispered.

"I'm not most guys."

A small burst of joy filled Emily's chest. He really *didn't* like Dominique! In fact, it seemed like Ben wanted nothing to do with her. It wasn't as good as finding out definitively that he liked Emily, but it did give her a certain guilty happiness. What was that SAT word she'd learned for taking delight in an enemy's unhappiness? *Schadenfreude?* She'd have to look that up when she got home.

Ben walked over to a sliding glass door with a small balcony on the other side. He opened the door and stepped out. She walked up next to him and looked down, where, fifteen feet below, the swimming pool shimmered in the moonlight. At the far end, a crowd of the Never Have I Ever players, including Spencer and Samantha, had stripped down to their underwear and were splashing each other and laughing.

"Be-en! Don't you want to at least see my dress?" shouted Dominique from behind them.

The night air blew cold against Emily's legs.

"Only one way out," said Ben as he started taking off his socks. "Know any sweet dives?"

Emily shook her head as Ben removed his shirt to reveal a thin yet muscular body.

"I'm a swimmer," Emily said. "Not a diver."

"Ben!" shouted Spencer from below. "Do a cannonball!" The rest of the crowd cheered and shouted Ben's name.

Emily tried to look away as he stripped down to his boxers. She ended up watching the far wall, where his projection pulled off its pajama bottoms and swung them playfully over its head several times while the crowd cheered.

"Right. Maybe just a standard flip for me," said Ben as he climbed over the edge of the balcony.

The crowd began to chant.

"Jump! Jump! Jump!"

Emily started to say, "This doesn't seem very sa—" But before she could finish her sentence, Ben was gone, flying through the air. He did a graceless flip and a half before landing in a near belly flop down below. The crowd exploded in applause.

A few seconds later, Ben surfaced and looked up at Emily.

"It's really nice in here!" he shouted. "You should come down!" He looked back at his friends and started to chant, "Em-i-ly! Em-i-ly!"

The others joined in. "Em-i-ly! Em-i-ly!"

"I don't have a suit!" she shouted at them, but the crowd only chanted louder.

"It's like that old song!" shouted Ben. "Come as you are!"

Emily looked down at her dress. She imagined the pool water soaking through the fabric and how much it would weigh as she tried to surface, how stupid she'd look with it fluttering around her on the way down, like a girlie pink-and-white parachute.

"Em-i-ly! Em-i-ly!"

She imagined what Ben would think of her if she didn't jump. Then she pictured opening the door to face a belligerent Dominique, and a shiver ran through her. She took off her shoes and swung her legs over the balcony. Ben looked up at her and smiled.

"I don't have any spare clothes!" she shouted at him.

"You can borrow some of mine!"

"We won't be able to get back into your room!" she warned.

"I'll pick the lock! Come on!"

She jumped.

For a moment, time froze as she hung in the night air, the pink ruffles of her skirt floating up past her waist, up to her shoulders. The crowd cheered and called her name as every pair of eyes followed her trajectory. And then, suddenly, the water parted beneath her feet and enveloped her.

She opened her eyes beneath the water's surface to see the soft pink of her dress, now darker with the wet, floating around her like candy-colored seaweed, and she wondered if there'd ever been a time in history when girls had to swim in long, flowing ball gowns. That definitely couldn't have been good for their race times.

As she began to push to the surface, she saw Ben swimming toward her, a big smile on his face. As he got closer, he put a hand on her shoulder and pulled his body close to hers. He closed his eyes and moved his lips close to Emily's.

Wait a second, she thought. *Is he trying to . . . to kiss me?*

A dozen pairs of legs kicked beneath the pool's surface a few feet away, and the sound of music and laughter filtered softly through the water. She wondered if anyone at the edge of the pool was looking down and watching them. This definitely wasn't what she'd had in mind when she'd imagined her first kiss.

Suddenly, Emily's head felt light, and she realized she hadn't taken a breath since she was up on Ben's balcony. She needed some air. Now. Two competing impulses took hold: Press her lips against Ben's or swim to the surface and breathe. A first kiss or oxygen? She wasn't sure which one she wanted more.

A moment passed, and Ben stayed in place, looking into her eyes and smiling. But he didn't move forward to kiss her, and after a few seconds, Emily's need to breathe grew so overwhelming that she had to swim to the surface.

A second later, Emily gulped air and treaded water as her dress floated up around her. She felt her now-exposed legs kicking through the water and tried to remember if she'd worn her stupid underwear with the pattern of kittens playing with balls of yarn.

She hoped that down below Ben was keeping his eyes closed and that he'd surface soon. After a few moments, he swam up beside her and inhaled deeply.

"Hey," he said. "What, uh, happened just then?"

"I needed a breath." She started swimming backward to the edge of the pool. "You didn't, uh, *look* while you were down there, did you?"

"I wouldn't dare, *kitten*," he said. "You wait here. I'll get you a towel and a change of clothes."

He pulled himself out of the pool and ran inside, his wet boxers clinging to his thighs as the nearby crowd whooped at him.

As Emily reached the pool's edge and struggled to heft

herself out, waterlogged dress and all, she looked up to see an angry stiletto-heeled figure staring down at her.

"At least now you'll have to change out of that stupid dress," whispered Dominique, crouching down and leaning over the pool but not offering Emily any help. "Don't think this means Ben is yours. Just because the two of you took a little swim—"

As Emily climbed farther out of the pool, Dominique tried to stand up, but her foot landed on Emily's soaked skirt and the wet taffeta slipped out from under her. She tried to steady herself, but it was no use. She stumbled forward over the ledge and into the pool.

Emily turned around to see a furious Dominique treading water. Her face was so angry and contorted that Emily felt an urge to call an exorcist. At the far end of the pool, Hannah, Amanda, and some of the other popular girls, who had witnessed the whole exchange, were laughing so hard they were crying.

"So that's how it's going to be," said Dominique.

"No, wait," said Emily. "I didn't mean—"

"Save it," said Dominique. "There's no stopping me now. I'm coming at you with everything I've got. Watch your back from here on out, Kessler. There's a target on it."

An hour later, Emily sat in the passenger seat of Samantha's truck—definitely not her first choice for a ride home, but Kimi and Phil had disappeared without warning, leaving Emily stranded, and Samantha had begrudgingly offered her a lift.

103

Normally, Emily's eyes would have bulged at the sight of the speedometer's needle pointing well past eighty, and her pulse would have quickened as the scenery rushed by, but tonight her only thoughts were of Ben Kale. She looked down to see the T-shirt and sweatpants he'd lent her, and a warm feeling radiated from her chest as she remembered jumping after him into the pool.

"What are you smiling about?" asked Samantha. "Your little boyfriend back at the party?"

"Ben's not my boyfriend," said Emily.

"Too bad," said Samantha. "You're kind of cute together."

"Really? You think so?"

Samantha rolled her eyes and muttered something that sounded like *freshmen*.

"Whatever," said Emily. "It doesn't matter. It's not like he'll actually ever be my boyfriend. It was fun hanging out, but I'm way too busy for, you know, date nights and going out to dinner and a movie, and dances and stuff."

"Too busy?" asked Samantha.

"My life—" started Emily. "It's scheduled down to the minute. I wake up, eat, head to school, swim for three hours, dinner, homework, stretching, maybe an hour to talk to people online, and then I'm so exhausted that I fall asleep the minute my head touches the pillow."

"It sounds like you've got a pretty packed schedule," said Samantha.

"Definitely."

"But on the other hand..." Samantha trailed off.

"What?"

"Well, you *did* make it out to the party tonight."

"This was a onetime thing."

"Right," said Samantha. "Of course."

Emily crossed her arms and glanced over at Samantha, trying to get a read on her. With her freshly shaved head and her motorcycle jacket, Samantha looked more like a heroine out of a postapocalyptic zombie movie than a high school girl. It was hard to believe they were talking about something as mundane as boys.

"Busy, busy girl," Samantha added.

"You're making fun of me," said Emily.

"You're pretty observant."

As they neared Emily's street, she told Samantha to stop and let her out a block from home.

"Daddy doesn't know you left?" asked Samantha.

"Does yours?"

Samantha shrugged and smiled. She pulled over to the street corner and killed the engine.

"Probably not," she admitted.

Emily opened the door and stepped out of the truck.

"Anyway," she said, "thanks for the ride."

She closed the door and had taken a few steps toward home when she heard Samantha's voice calling after her.

"Hey, Kessler! If your sister had time for a boyfriend, so do you."

Emily turned to respond, but by the time the words had sunk in, Samantha's engine had already roared to life. In all her years around a pool, Emily had only belly flopped off a diving board once or twice. Now, she had that same feeling, as if all the air had been pushed out of her.

"Your sister had time for a boyfriend."

Emily watched in silence as the older girl's taillights disappeared into the distance.

"Your sister had...a boyfriend."

It was impossible, right, to live in the same house as someone for more than a dozen years without really knowing her? And yet—Emily's parents knew nothing about Ben. Emily had never mentioned him, and she'd sneaked out to his party without them knowing. Was it possible that Emily herself had been just as clueless about Sara's love life?

Emily turned and started walking home, the words echoing in her mind. What if what Samantha had said was true? What did it mean if Sara—the Machine—turned out to have been human?

CHAPTER EIGHT

Halfway through her 10K run the next morning, Emily was starting to regret going to Ben's party. What was the point in trying to get together with a cute guy if she collapsed and died of a heart attack by the side of the road before she even got a kiss?

"You're almost a minute over your usual time at the 5K mark!" her father shouted from the driver's seat of his car. On Saturdays, he liked to drive at her side as she ran her circuit through sleepy suburban neighborhoods. "I sure hope you're planning to pick it up in the back half of the run."

"When's the last time you even ran a mile?" Emily said under her breath.

"What's that?" her dad barked. "I couldn't quite hear you.

Sounds like you're a little winded!" He reached over to his CD player and switched it on. "Maybe this will fire you up."

"Dad, no," Emily said, her lungs burning as she tried to speed up her pace. "Please don't. It's *way* too early in the morning for this."

"Too late!" her dad said, smiling gleefully.

A few seconds later, the national anthem started playing.

"Please stop," Emily said, barely able to talk and breathe at the same time.

"You've got to visualize!" her dad shouted. "You're on top of the Olympic podium, the flag unfurled behind you...and then 'The Star-Spangled Banner' starts blasting from the stadium's speakers!"

"This isn't...helping," said Emily. Her legs felt like jelly as each step of the run sent a shock wave through her aching muscles.

"Out in the crowd are the girls you beat. The Brazilians, the Australians. The Canadians! Yeah, that's right. We're not listening to 'O Canada,' Em. Those are the Stars and Stripes hanging at your back. That's *our* anthem playing!"

She tried to ignore the blaring music and the pain and sleepiness. That's what Sara would do: Fight through it all and find a way to speed up and beat her usual time. Sara would find a way to win.

And then Emily remembered: *"Your sister had...a boyfriend."*

The sentence sat in Emily's gut like a stone she'd swallowed and couldn't digest. She needed to find out more about this supposed boyfriend, preferably soon. Suddenly, every conversation she'd had with the upperclassmen had taken on a new shade of meaning. Phil had mentioned knowing Sara, and Samantha claimed to know about some kind of secret boyfriend—but it was Cameron Clark who *kept* talking about Sara. When Emily had told him that Sara had never mentioned his name, he'd seemed so— disappointed.

"Dad," she said, "did you ever see any guys hanging out with Sara?"

"What?" he asked. "I can't hear you!"

"Maybe turn the music down a little?"

He shook his head. "In the middle of the national anthem?" He turned the volume up. Maybe it had been pointless to ask, anyway. Emily had a feeling he'd chosen not to hear on purpose.

"...And the rockets' red glare," her father sang along with the car stereo, "the bombs bursting in air!"

She couldn't stand it anymore. Emily quickened her pace, almost sprinting as she tried to get as far away from him as possible.

"Yeah!" her dad exclaimed as he accelerated to catch up. "That's the spirit!"

That night, Kimi came by for their monthly sleepover. She unpacked her never-to-be-mentioned-to-anyone-on-pain-of-death Hello Kitty sleeping bag as Emily sorted through her friend requests on Facebook, trying to figure out which people she actually knew. Kimi kicked off her shoes and flopped facedown on Emily's bed.

"Uh, so, sorry about last night," said Kimi, avoiding eye contact.

"No problem. I got a ride home from Samantha," said Emily as her cursor hovered over Zach Reynolds's friend request. They *had* played Never Have I Ever together. Technically, that qualified as a kind of friendship, right? She hit Accept.

"Kimi, I know this might sound weird, but have you ever heard any rumors? Like, about my sister?"

Kimi sat up and looked over at her.

"About Sara? No. I mean, I doubt anyone would say anything to me. They know you and I are friends. Honestly, though, I don't think there's much to say."

"Yeah," said Emily. "You're probably right. Sorry I brought it up."

It doesn't matter, she thought. *I'm pretty sure I know who I need to talk to anyway.*

She imagined what it would feel like to confront Cameron Clark, to ask him if he and Sara had secretly dated. A shiver went through her as she turned back to the computer.

"Let's talk about something else," she added after a few seconds. "Something fun."

Kimi flipped onto her back and let her head roll over the edge of the bed. Her hair hung down like thin black icicles as she arched her back like a contented cat and looked expectantly at Emily.

"Okay," she said. "Ask me about my night."

"Huh? What about it?"

"Emily! Try to keep up with me on this," she said. "I mean, I disappear from a party with one of the hottest, most popular guys in school, who also happens to be totally nice and who *also* has an awesome car, and you're not even *curious*?"

"Okay, so, what happened?" asked Emily, swiveling her chair to look at Kimi.

"Oh, I don't know," Kimi said. "I'm not one to kiss and tell."

Emily shrugged and turned her attention back to the computer.

"What are you doing?!" asked Kimi. "Don't you want to know about me and Phil?"

Emily turned back to her. "But you just said—"

"I can't just *tell* you what happened. It would be—unladylike. But maybe if you begged me a little, and promised never to tell anyone, and offered to reveal all your darkest secrets, and threatened to torture the information out of me—"

"Fine," said Emily. "Tell me what happened or I'll—I'll tell everyone at school that you have lice. And a fake leg. And that you have an entire wall of Justin Bieber posters in your room."

Kimi put a hand over her mouth in mock horror.

"You wouldn't," she said.

"Oh, I would."

"Well, then, I guess I'll have to confess," said Kimi. "But I want it noted that anything I tell you is entirely off the record, and that I shared it with you under duress."

"Noted."

"So *maybe* Phil drove me to the lake, and *maybe* he and I kind of sort of made out in his car. For four hours."

"What?!"

"Yes!"

"For *four* hours?" asked Emily.

Kimi nodded, then grabbed Emily's pillow and fell back on the bed, screaming gleefully into it.

"*Four* hours," said Emily.

Kimi removed the pillow just long enough to say, "I know! I know!"

"Was it—good?"

"Well, yeah," said Kimi. "Except now my lips are *really* chapped. But I haven't even told you the best part yet!"

"What?"

"He totally asked me to homecoming!"

"What?!"

"So maybe we could make it a double date?" asked Kimi. "Like—with me and Phil. And you and Ben."

Kimi looked hopefully at Emily, who was sitting, mouth open, trying to process this request. A week ago, the whole scenario would have seemed impossible—the two of them heading to homecoming with a couple of the most popular guys at school. Now it all seemed suddenly real, tangible even, as if the Ben that Emily had dreamed about holding at night could reach out and wrap his arms around her.

"Kimi—you know I can't."

"I do?" Kimi asked. She sat on the edge of the bed, coyly crossing her legs, and put her elbow on her knee. Then she leaned forward, put her chin on her fist, and looked at Emily with a puzzled expression on her face. "Explain."

"Well, for one, there's my dad. Never in a million years would he let me go to a dance. And then there's Ben Kale. He hasn't exactly asked me."

"Em, you're killing me."

Kimi flopped back down on the bed and covered her face with her hands.

"There's no way I can go," said Emily.

Kimi started to make hacking noises as if she were gasping her last breaths.

"I'm—dying here. Don't—do this—to me!" She rolled to one side and looked up pleadingly. "You do *want* to go, right?"

For a moment, Emily closed her eyes and pictured Ben in a suit, roses cleverly hidden behind his back, ringing her doorbell to pick her up for the dance. She imagined him offering her an arm, walking her out to his car, and opening the door for her. She imagined dancing to the last song of the night with him as he looked down into her eyes, and then letting him walk her up to her doorstep and leaning in and—

Okay, yeah. She *did* want to go.

"Fine! If I happen to see Ben, and the subject of homecoming *happens* to come up, then I'll see what I can do."

Kimi sprang to her feet and pulled Emily from her chair. She took Emily's hands and started mock slow-dancing with her, twirling her around and humming an old R&B song.

"This is going to be amazing," said Kimi.

"He hasn't even asked me y—"

Kimi shushed her.

"Going. To. Be. Amazing."

On Sunday, Emily went to bed at her usual time. As she closed her eyes, she wondered if she'd see Ben the next day. It hadn't been until she got home from his party that she'd realized she hadn't given him her number or even an e-mail address.

Of course, if Ben had really wanted to track her down, he could have found her on Facebook or asked around until he found a way to contact her. Did that mean he wasn't really that interested? Maybe the moment they'd shared at the party had been just that: a moment, a tiny, magical parcel of time that was now over.

Restless, she turned to look at the clock and read 10:42. How could she possibly be having trouble sleeping when she was still exhausted from staying up so late on Friday? If anything, she should have gone to sleep hours ago to make up for it. Was worrying about a guy really enough to throw off the sleep schedule she'd carefully cultivated for almost three years?

Stupid boys. Stupid Ben. Stupid her for caring. Stupid tapping sound at the window. How was she supposed to sleep with that—

Stupid tapping sound at the window?

She rolled out of bed, walked quietly over to the window, and raised the blind to reveal a figure in a dark hoodie. She almost screamed before she looked down at the figure's arms and realized what he was carrying: her dress from Friday.

"Ben?" she asked, opening her window.

He removed his hoodie, which upon closer examination read GO LIZARDS!, and stepped inside.

"What are you, a ninja now?" she asked as he handed her the dress.

"A ninja who delivers dry cleaning," he said. "Actually, ninja is kind of an exaggeration. The tree outside your window is pretty easy to climb."

"What are you doing here?"

He looked down at the dress and asked, "Isn't it obvious?" as he handed it to her.

"Well, thanks," she said. "But you could have just given it to me at school."

"I figured this would be a good excuse to come see you. Maybe we could go get some coffee or something."

"Right now? I'm about to go to sleep."

"Thus the coffee. It'll wake you up."

"You're serious?" she asked.

"I'm *always* serious."

"No, you're not."

"Well, I am this time."

Emily thought about tomorrow. She had an Honors History test and a brutal private swim practice scheduled, *and* her dad had been watching her suspiciously ever since that jog on Saturday, despite the fact that she'd finished only fifteen seconds over her usual time.

Her arguments for telling him to leave weighed like bags full of iron on one side of a scale. On the other side, though, was Ben. Ben, who had driven all the way across town to return her dress. Who looked especially cute in his school hoodie.

"You're going to have to go outside," she said, and his face fell. Then she smiled and added, "So I can get changed."

Twenty minutes later, Ben and Emily walked into Hallowed Grounds, a twenty-four-hour coffee-and-doughnut shop that Emily had jogged by several dozen times but never imagined she'd go inside. Coffee stunted your growth. Doughnuts were empty calories. Neither fit into the system Emily's father had created for her. But then again, neither did Ben Kale.

"Okay, since you're a coffee rookie, I'm recommending we start you off with a mocha—and lots of milk," said Ben, as he ordered for them. "I'll be sticking with my usual triple espresso."

A few minutes later, the barista handed Emily a steaming mug and she tried her first sip of coffee. Ben looked at her expectantly.

"What do you think?"

She grimaced. "It's like poisoned hot chocolate."

"It's an acquired taste."

They took their cups to the back of the shop and sat in old red-velvet-covered armchairs whose fabric was worn from

116

years of use. As bad as the coffee tasted, Emily had to admit that she loved the smell, and after a few sips she learned to ignore the bitterness and concentrate on the chocolate.

"So," Ben said, "here we are. Out past your bedtime on a school night."

"Heh," she said, looking down at her cup. "Yeah."

Ben sipped his drink. It was the first time since she'd met him that she'd felt a lull in their usual banter. The silence wasn't uncomfortable, though. If anything, it felt kind of nice.

"You're kind of always—*on*, aren't you?" she asked after a second.

"What do you mean?"

"You're always joking, entertaining people."

"Thank you?"

"Don't get me wrong, I like that you're funny. But sometimes, don't you feel like it's nice to slow down and just talk without all that pressure to be witty?" Emily didn't have much practice making conversation alone with boys, let alone on dates, but something about Ben's easygoing nature made her feel like she could say anything. She wanted to know everything about him.

"Huh," he said, looking a bit lost in thought.

"What's with that shelf of trophies?" asked Emily. "You were so—I don't know—elusive the other night. What made you stop competing?"

"Nothing specific, really," said Ben, sinking deeper into his chair. "Well, I guess, like a year ago, my parents split up, but that isn't what made me stop trying to win science fairs."

"Oh, I'm sorry," said Emily. She felt bad—Ben looked so uncomfortable now. Maybe she'd pushed him too far. "That must have been tough."

"Yeah," said Ben. "I don't know. I don't blame my mom for leaving. By the time she took off, my dad was basically living at Lowman-Howe—that's the chemical company he works for. He's just that kind of guy. He'd rather be in his lab than back at home. Even when he is around, he's always at his computer or checking his BlackBerry."

"What about your mom?"

"She's kind of the opposite. She's all about yoga and eating vegan and 'finding herself.' She moved to New York for good when she split up with my dad." He looked up at Emily. "What about you? What's your family like?"

"My mom's pretty cool," Emily started, figuring she'd save talking about her dad for later. No need to scare Ben off on the first date. Was this even an official date? "She's an elementary school teacher, so she was great when my sister and I were little." She regretted the words as soon as they came out of her mouth. Why had she mentioned Sara? She just hoped he wouldn't ask anything more about—

"What was she like?" he asked. "Your sister, I mean. I met her a couple of times, but I never really got to know her."

Emily looked down at her drink. What was there to say? If what Samantha had said the other day was true, maybe Emily didn't know anything about Sara at all. For a second, she thought about telling him "I don't know," but then she thought better of it. For now, it was better not to open that door.

"She was great," she said. "She was a hero to me. She was going to grow up and win every medal out there. And then she got in a car with that stupid boy, and then—" Her hands were shaking. "You work so hard for something, and then it gets taken away in an instant."

"What happened?" Ben asked. He reached out and took her hand. "I don't really know all the details."

"It was a rainy night. Sara had stayed late at the pool to go swimming. The guy, Nick Brown—he's a yearbook photographer, so he stayed with her to take some pictures. She was supposed to run home as part of her training regimen, but instead she ended up getting a ride from him. He crashed less than a mile from my house. He was fine. She wasn't."

"I'm sorry," he said. "I mean, I was pretty upset when my mom left, but at least she wasn't—"

"Yeah."

She wished she could just talk about her sister's death like a normal person. But she couldn't. The thought of it always reminded her of the simple fact that the universe wasn't fair. A girl could spend her whole life preparing for races she'd never get to swim. A random stranger could get her killed and still end up roaming the halls of her high school a few months later, taking pictures for the stupid yearbook.

"Please," she said. "Say something. Anything. Talk about something different."

"I, uh—" She could tell he was thinking about making a joke. But he must have changed his mind, because instead he said, "I almost went with my mom when she left. But I didn't. I think she assumed I'd follow her wherever she went, and when that turned out to be false, it really hurt her."

As he spoke, Emily felt her body stop shaking and her breathing return to normal. She liked the sound of his voice. She felt calm in its presence.

"She thought I'd chosen my dad over her, but that wasn't it. I just figured I'd rather stick around here, closer to my friends."

"Yeah," said Emily. "I can see that. I don't know what I'd do if I had to move away from Kimi."

Thinking of Kimi, Emily suddenly remembered homecoming and the promise she'd made. Her mind raced, turning over ways she might hint that she wanted Ben to ask her to the dance. It was nice to have a new, normal agenda for this conversation, something to put Sara out of her mind.

"Kimi seems like a fun girl," said Ben. "I heard she and Phil have been, uh, hanging out lately."

Emily could barely believe it. This was a perfect opening.

"Yeah," she said. "Phil actually asked her to go to homecoming. Now it's all she can talk about."

"That's funny," said Ben, sipping his espresso. "Some girls get so excited about a stupid dance."

"You think homecoming is stupid?"

"Well, yeah," he said. "Homecoming is basically just a party with no drinking, censored music, and no hooking up."

120

He stared down at his now-empty cup. "Plus," he added, "I'm not exactly *allowed* to go to homecoming. I'm on academic probation, so I'm not allowed to participate in any school activities until I get my grades up, and I don't see *that* happening anytime soon."

So that was it. It wasn't that Ben didn't *want* to go to homecoming. It was that he *couldn't*.

"Is it really so impossible for you to do better in your classes?"

"Considering I never do any homework, don't study, and rarely show up to class, I'd say it's unlikely my grades are going to improve in the near future," he said, grinning.

Suddenly, though, Ben's smile seemed like an act, communicating nothing about what he was actually feeling. The smile was a wall, protecting him. Earlier, for a moment, when they were talking about their families, it had felt as if the wall was crumbling. Now it was back, higher than ever. Could she really be with someone like that? Someone whose real thoughts she could never know? That easy, comfortable feeling she'd had just moments ago had vanished.

"It's late," she said. "I should probably go."

"I said something wrong, didn't I?"

"No, no," Emily lied. "I'm just tired."

They spent most of the car ride home in silence. Emily looked out the window, trying not to think of crashing and hoping to avoid eye contact with Ben. On the way to the coffee shop, she'd been so excited to hop into a car with him that she hadn't really considered the danger. Now, that excitement had waned. A week ago, if you had asked her to imagine a bad date with Ben Kale, she would have thought it was impossible. Now, suddenly, she was living one out.

"Emily—" Ben said as they reached her block.

"What?"

"You want to go to that dance."

She sneaked a glance at him and saw a worried look on his face. She shrugged.

"Maybe."

"What if it was possible?" he asked as he pulled over to the side of the street near her house.

"Like what? You somehow change straight F's into A's in the next few weeks?"

"Yeah," he said. "Something like that."

"And you'd be doing this just so you can take me to a 'stupid dance'?"

"That would be the idea, yes."

"And you really think you can do it?"

He hesitated for a second, and she could almost see the gears turning in his brain as he attempted to come up with some cocky remark. Finally, though, he just said, "I can try."

She turned to look at him again and found him leaning forward. He reached out with one hand, ran it through her hair, and rested it behind her head. Then he closed his eyes and moved closer. He started pulling her in.

This was it. Her first kiss. Except—except, could she really do it? Did Ben even know she'd never kissed anyone? Emily's heart began to race from a combination of her first taste of coffee and the very real possibility of her first kiss. What if she was terrible and he thought she was just naturally bad, when really it was because she'd never had any practice? Should he at least know what he was getting into?

"Wait," she said, and Ben opened his eyes.

"Is something wrong?"

"I've just—I've never—"

"Oh!" he said. "You've never—" He kept his hand where it was, behind her head, and looked into her eyes. "Well, then, your first kiss should be special."

"It should?" she asked. "I mean, yes. It should."

"So we'll wait," he said. "For the right moment."

"Like maybe," she said, a smile breaking across her face, "until the dance."

He took a deep breath and leaned back into his seat. His eyes never left her, and Emily wondered if anyone had ever looked at her so intently.

"Until the dance," he said. "Well, then, maybe I actually *will* be looking forward to homecoming."

CHAPTER
NINE

That Thursday, the Twin Branches swim team prepared for its first meet of the year, an exhibition match against its crosstown rivals, the Wilson High Badgers. Of course, all the girls on the team knew that the real competition wasn't between the two schools at all; it was between Emily and Dominique.

As Emily tightened her swim cap and rubbed a smudge from her goggles, Dominique approached. She walked jerkily, keeping her joints stiff as she moved.

"Hello. Swim. Bot! Are you. Ready. To. Lose?"

Other girls in the locker room glanced over and shook their heads.

"Don't be mean," said Amanda. "You're making fun of her—and robots!"

"Seriously," said Hannah. "Kessler is cool in my book.

Did you see her the other night, jumping into the pool after Ben?"

"I jumped into the pool, too," said Dominique, her face growing red.

"More like fell," said Hannah, smiling.

"She fell?" asked another girl, who had just walked in. "Wish I could have seen that. I guess I was distracted, watching Ben run around in his boxers."

"Speaking of which," said Amanda, turning to Emily. "Are you two dating now?"

"Maybe?" said Emily, genuinely unsure.

"If you don't know, you're not dating," said Dominique as she turned to leave. Once she was safely out of the room, Hannah came over and sat next to Emily.

"Don't listen to her," said Hannah. "I've had two-year relationships where the guy never admitted we were a couple."

Emily felt a strange mix of emotions: first, happiness that the other girls had jumped to her aid and taken an interest in her relationship with Ben, but second, fear. What if her dad heard the girls talking like this? If he found out about Ben, who knew what would happen? Homecoming would be a no-go—not to mention any hope of a social life ever again.

"Hey, guys? Can we, uh, keep all this stuff with Ben a secret for now?" Emily asked. "We're still figuring things out."

"Say no more," said Hannah. "You can't be too careful. People want to know if you're officially together, and then *you* feel like you have to know. And sometimes having that define-the-relationship talk turns into an end-the-relationship one."

"Uh, yeah," said Emily. She hoped Hannah and the other girls really would keep quiet about this. That was possible, right? Right?

Maybe it was best not to think about it.

A few minutes later, Emily waited on top of lane four's starting block. Dominique stood a few feet away in lane two. The first race was the 100-meter freestyle, an event that Dominique typically dominated.

Emily glanced over at her rival, trying to get a read on her, but Dominique just stared down the lane, focused solely on the water.

Emily looked across the pool toward the bleachers, where a larger-than-usual crowd had gathered. She recognized a few faces from the party: Zach, Marcus, Kevin, and Amir, not to mention Phil, who sat next to Kimi, holding her hand. Today, Kimi's hair was done up in a bunch of impossibly tight pin curls, secured with floral clips. Emily guessed it was an homage to retro swim caps. And next to Kimi was Ben. He was sitting right in the center of the top row, holding a posterboard sign reading GO EMILY!

Seeing the sign made her smile and simultaneously hope it wouldn't raise her dad's suspicions. Luckily for Emily, Coach Kessler was staring at her instead. Dressed in the same dark gray suit he'd worn to races for the past ten years, now too tight around his increasingly chubby frame, he stood motionless, his eyes fixed on Emily. As the race time neared and she bent down to grip the underside of the starting block, his eyes never left her while he silently evaluated her stance. If she had even one finger or toe out of place, she'd hear about it later.

"Em-i-ly!" Ben shouted. "Em-i-ly!"

It was just like back at the party, when he'd chanted her name to make her jump into the pool. And just like back at the party, the other students joined in. Zach and Marcus, Phil and Kimi, and other kids she didn't even know; they were all rooting for her. A month ago, the entire team had cheered against her as Emily lost a race to Dominique. Now the tables were turned.

Emily looked over to see Dominique listening to the crowd's chant and shaking with anger. Good. Now it was her turn to be distracted.

Emily focused back on the race just in time. The starting bell chimed, and she leaped forward into the water. Short freestyle races like this were all about power—going full-out for a single minute and knowing just how far you could push your body before it broke down.

Emily thrashed through the water, touched the far wall, and kick-flipped to head back in the opposite direction. The crowd continued to cheer, and the sound of her own name filled Emily's ears, urging her forward. She flew down the lane and kicked off the wall again. The crowd's chanting infused her with a new kind of energy, one she hadn't felt before, as if each voice were a hand pushing her forward.

As she reached the final lap of the race, the one where her muscles usually burned with exhaustion, she felt a surge of adrenaline. She wouldn't lose this time. Not in front of people who were cheering her name. Not in front of Ben.

She kicked her legs and pulled at the water with her arms. And then suddenly, she reached forward and felt the grain of the pool wall against her fingertips. A cheer rose through the gym, and the announcer called out, "With a time of one minute, four-point-three seconds, Kessler is the winner!"

The freestyle win was the first of many. Not only did Emily beat Dominique in breaststroke and butterfly like usual, she even beat her in backstroke. Emily won every heat of every race. She dominated, and with each win, the crowd chanted her name even louder.

When the event was finally over, the crowd surrounded Emily, congratulating her and requesting her presence at post-meet meals. In the distance, she saw Dominique, her shoulders pulled back tight, refusing to look defeated as she escaped the crowd and retreated into the locker room. Emily almost felt bad for her. Almost.

The crowd parted as Ben approached.

"Em!" he said. "You were unbelievable!"

He reached in and tried to give her a hug, but she pulled away and glanced meaningfully over at her dad, who was watching everything.

"Not right now," she said, and Ben frowned. "Sorry," she added, remembering she'd never told him about her dad's no-dating policy. "I'll explain later."

"Yeah, Em, sure," he said. "I'm just gonna, you know, take

off, then. I'll see you at school tomorrow." He backed away. She wished she could explain it all—that the reason she wasn't throwing her arms around him was *because* she liked him so much and wanted to keep seeing him, but there was just no way, not with all of these people around.

He took another step back, and the crowd closed around Emily, sealing her away from him.

On the drive home, Emily's dad was quieter than usual. Normally, he'd spend this time picking apart her performances—her millisecond-late start on the breaststroke or her overly conservative pace on the 200-meter butterfly. Today, though, he said nothing. Could it really be that he had nothing to criticize? Finally, he broke the silence.

"Seems like you had quite a few *fans* out there," he said.

Panic gripped Emily. Did he know she'd sneaked out to go to the party? Did he know about Ben?

"The, uh, article really won some people over," she said.

He nodded, seemingly accepting her explanation.

"You must be feeling pretty proud of yourself for winning like that," he said. "But I wonder if you happened to notice your race times?"

Though Emily had beaten Dominique in each race and felt good while she was swimming, her times had indeed been unexceptional. If anything, she was a few tenths of a second off her usual pace in most of the races.

"You won because Dominique had an off day," her dad continued. "Not because of anything you did."

"I won. She lost," said Emily. "If you need to yell at someone, yell at her."

"I'm not yelling," he said. "I'm trying to warn you. This was just an exhibition swim. It didn't count for anything. For all you know, she didn't swim her hardest. Two weeks from now, though, are Quals for Junior Nationals. Those are the races that *do* count. Those are the races you want to win."

"Why can't you just let me have this?" she asked. "Why can't you just let me feel good about winning this one?"

In truth, she *didn't* feel good, and the worst thing was, she didn't quite know why. She had everything she wanted, didn't she? The crowd had cheered for her—Ben had even made her a sign—and she'd beaten Dominique in every race. So why did she feel so hollow?

Because it was built on deception, all of it. The moment her dad found out about her new friends or her dates with Ben, he'd put a stop to everything. She'd be grounded, monitored at all times, probably even in her sleep. If there was a way for her dad to get inside her dreams and watch her there, he'd find it.

And if she got caught, she'd be right back where she had started: nearly friendless and utterly single.

"Being a champion means winning when it matters," her dad said after a few seconds. "Sara set her record at Junior Nationals. And she needed every millisecond of that time to edge out Amy—Willings? Williams? The second-place girl. No one remembers *her* name."

Emily had heard this speech a thousand times before, and

she tuned out as her dad spoke. She felt empty, her guts scraped out like a jack-o'-lantern's. There was no certainty, no stability. Her new life seemed destined to crumble at the slightest touch. Worst of all, Emily couldn't imagine a future where things were any different. What if she couldn't be happy, no matter what? Even when she won, she couldn't win.

"Disaster!" said Kimi the next day as she walked on a treadmill next to Emily in the high school weight room, dressed head to toe in black and white, right down to her pristine Chuck Taylors. "I'm starting to think I shouldn't go to the dance with Phil!" Around them, other girls pretended to lift weights while they talked about potential homecoming dates.

In the meantime, Emily was going at a full sprint on her treadmill, barely able to breathe. She managed to take a gulp of air and ask, "What happened?"

"Since we've been hanging out, I've been learning all kinds of things about Phil that I've been adding to his spreadsheet," said Kimi. "Like did you know he used to date Mallika? Or that he spends an hour gelling his hair every morning?"

"Huh," said Emily as she turned her treadmill's pace from "sprint" to "jog" so she could cool down.

"And in the meantime, *Marcus's* spreadsheet is looking better and better! Like did you know he's going to be in a bathing-suit ad for this clothing catalog? Well, not his face, but you'll be able to see his abs and one of his legs."

"That's cool," said Emily. "But what about Phil? Aren't those two friends?"

"It'll be hard," said Kimi. "But Phil will get over it. I'm going to have to tell him it's over. We've had a lot of fun together, and I'll always look back on our relationship fondly, but—"

"You've been together for, like, a week!"

"Has it been that long already?" asked Kimi. "I'd better get this over with so I can let Marcus know I'm available for the dance. Oh! Speaking of homecoming, have you talked with Ben yet?"

"Yeah," said Emily.

"And?"

"And he wants to take me."

"Em!" Kimi shouted. "That's amazing! I'd give you a hug if you weren't totally covered in sweat."

"Thanks."

"I don't know how you can stay so calm at a time like this," said Kimi. "All of your hard work is *finally* paying off! People are really starting to recognize how great you are. The coolest guy in school is taking you to homecoming, and your best friend is going to the dance with her choice of hotties."

Kimi was right. It *sounded* like the perfect life. But didn't Kimi realize how doomed it all was? Emily felt like a passenger on a train who had seen the bridge out ahead, except that if she tried to tell everyone around her, they'd just assume she was being silly.

But it was true. Her dad *would* find out, and he'd happily knock her new life to pieces as if it were a piñata. Emily took a breath. Maybe it was time to discuss all this. Rationally, if possible.

"I guess—" she started. "I guess I'm just worried my dad is going to find out about everything."

"He won't."

"How do you know?"

"Because people around here value their lives way too much to mess with my best friend," said Kimi. "If anyone says a peep about Ben or the dance to your dad, I'll kill 'em."

"You're sweet," said Emily, less reassured than ever.

Kimi smiled. "Don't forget 'and deadly.' Now stop worrying so much, remember to smile, and mark your calendar. In a couple Saturdays, dress shopping at the mall. We can tell your dad we're working on a science project."

"You think he'll buy that?"

"Of course he will," said Kimi. "You're his perfect little daughter. You never lie."

Kimi was right, of course. Emily's dad would believe her, and he'd keep believing her over and over again. Until she got caught once.

For now, the only thing Emily could do was make sure that never happened.

Kimi sometimes asked Emily if she felt scared swimming alone in the pool after her dad left or jogging home by herself. In truth, Emily never felt unsafe. This was the kind of town where no one ever got mugged, and kids stealing a lawn gnome topped the Crime Blotter section of the newspaper.

That changed after school one night the next week, when Emily saw a lanky figure dressed in black on the other side of the indoor pool's glass wall. The figure moved to the doorway, found it open, and slowly turned the handle as Emily swam to the far end of the pool.

As the door opened, she got out and wrapped herself in a towel, figuring that if this guy was some kind of killer, she could run out the back. Then, as the door opened, she saw that it was Nick Brown.

For a moment, they stared at each other from opposite sides of the pool. Though she was used to being in a bathing suit, Emily had never felt so naked.

"What are you doing here?" she shouted after a few seconds.

"I just—" he started. "I just—"

"Get out!" she screamed. "Get out! Get out! Get out!"

"Please," he said. "Don't—"

But she didn't want to hear it. She backed away and fled into the girls' locker room, where she knew he wouldn't follow. Once she was inside, she ran into a bathroom stall and tucked her feet up with her on the toilet seat so that even if he did come in, he wouldn't find her.

It was only after a few minutes had passed that Emily began to regret running away. Sure, he was a guy, but he hadn't seemed hostile and he was far less muscular than she was— not much of a physical threat at all. And as much as she hated him, she had questions she wanted to ask.

Like why had he given Sara a ride home that day?

What had they talked about?

And had she mentioned any boyfriends? Cameron Clark, for example? Something wasn't adding up. Was Cameron somehow also involved in the crash? Maybe he and Sara had fought, which made her want to leave school with Nick, or maybe—

Nick was right on the other side of the locker-room doors, Emily realized. She could get answers now.

But by the time she walked back out, Nick was gone. The pool sat empty, its water still as ice.

At lunch the next day, as Emily took her usual spot at the center table, Kimi gestured to the corner of the cafeteria. There, sitting by herself, wearing a thick pair of headphones and drinking a protein shake in place of her usual junk food, was Dominique. She wore no makeup, was dressed in a tracksuit, and looked like she hadn't brushed her hair since last week's swim meet.

"Where's her sidekick?" asked Kimi before noticing Lindsay at the next table over, talking with Spencer. "And what's she doing over in our old spot? Did she take last week's loss as a sign that she permanently belongs in Loserville?"

"Maybe I should go talk to her," said Emily. "I feel bad."

"Are you insane?" asked Kimi. "We finally get to enjoy a lunch in peace without her making fun of us every five seconds, and you want to go make nice?"

"I'm just going to say hi."

She chose not to mention another agenda: finding out

where Cameron was eating lunch today. She'd been wanting to track him down since Ben's party, but the task had proved difficult, and Emily was beginning to suspect that he was avoiding her on purpose.

Emily walked over to Dominique's table only to find herself completely ignored. Dominique listened to her headphones, sipped from her shake, and stared into space. She didn't notice Emily until she waved a hand in front of Dominique's face.

"What do you want, Kessler?" she asked.

"I was just, uh, worried that you—"

Dominique paused her iPod, took off her headphones, and sneered. "Good," she said. "You should be worried."

"I should?"

"You really taught me something," said Dominique. "I used to make fun of you for being a Swimbot. Now I see that you just wanted to win at any cost, even if it meant sacrificing everything else. I respect that."

"Thanks?" said Emily. What was Dominique getting at?

"So I just want you to know that I'm coming at you full-on now," said Dominique. "I started a new eating plan, and I'm adding another hour of practice to my normal routine. I'm done with parties, drinking, staying out late, all of it. There's no point in doing that stuff anyway. I won't be happy until I destroy you at Junior Nationals."

"I—" Emily had no idea how to respond.

"Now if you don't mind, I'd appreciate it if you'd get out of here," said Dominique. "I've got the full lunch hour scheduled to listen to this podcast about positive visualization, and you're kind of eating into my time."

Dominique put her headphones back on and resumed staring into space as Emily stood there, wordless. She kicked herself for not asking about Cameron earlier—there was no way she was going to do it now. Finally, she turned and rejoined Kimi at the center table.

"Well," asked Kimi. "What did she say?"

"She's becoming..." Emily trailed off. "She's becoming *me*."

In study hall that day, as Emily struggled through her Statistics homework, Ben sat down at the desk next to her and leaned over to whisper, "Hey."

"What are you doing here?" she asked. "Shouldn't you be, you know, in class?"

"I told Mr. Carr I had appendicitis. Again. He really is a terrible health teacher."

"I thought you were supposed to be working on your grades," said Emily with a frown. Had he just told her that in the heat of the moment? What if he hadn't changed at all? Her mom had warned her about guys like Ben, guys who promised girls the world at night and then took it all back the next morning.

"I am. I really am," he said. "I already turned in the last month and a half's worth of calculus problem sets, and I just got 105 percent on my AP Physics test. But is everything still okay with you? Last week at the pool you acted like I was a creepy stranger or something."

Emily was about to reply when Mrs. Watanabe walked by, checking to make sure everyone was still hard at work. She grabbed an iPhone away from Howard Wu, who was in the process of burning down his Sims' house, and stuck it in her pocket. Emily and Ben waited in silence until she'd returned to her desk before resuming their conversation.

"I just want to keep things between us—private. At least for now."

"You're embarrassed of me?"

"What? No, of course not."

He raised an eyebrow. "I mean, we've only been on one date," he said. "I think it's a little early for us to start fighting."

"No, I'm not embarrassed about you—us—whatever," said Emily.

"Good," he said. "Because I already told Spencer about our late-night rendezvous, and he's not exactly the best at keeping secrets."

Emily cringed. What if Spencer had blabbed to Lindsay? Or even worse, Dominique?

"The thing is, I may have forgotten to mention that my dad is kind of a controlling psycho who'll ground me for life if he finds out I'm secretly dating you."

"So we're 'dating' now?" asked Ben.

"Are you kidding me?" asked Emily. "Did you just hear a word I said?"

"Emily, you worry too much," said Ben. "Not getting caught is my specialty. I've sneaked you out after bedtime once. There's no reason to think I can't do it again. And again. And again."

"This is going to end badly," said Emily.

"Is that a reason not to try?"

She looked into his brown eyes and suddenly lost her ability to say no. She'd have to work on that.

"I guess I wouldn't be *upset* if you happened to show up at ten thirty tonight," she said.

"Sounds good. I'll send you a text when I get to your place. Then you can just hop out the window and"—footsteps approached—"yes, that *is* how you get the derivative of that equation! Thanks for the help."

Emily looked over her shoulder to see Mrs. Watanabe lurking behind her.

"Kale, out," she said. "Kessler, save the romance for your own time. I'd hate to tell your father that you're sitting out a meet to head to detention, but I'll risk it if I have to."

"See you tonight," mouthed Ben silently as he backed out of the room, and Emily couldn't help but smile. He was right. Even if it was doomed to fail, even if it was only a matter of time, seeing him was worth it. She had to try.

CHAPTER TEN

Over the course of the next week, Emily and Ben developed a routine. At ten thirty, she'd say good night to her parents, turn off her light, and lock her door. By ten thirty-five, he'd text her to say he'd arrived, and by ten forty, she'd be walking down the block, bundled up in a huge coat to keep out the cold November air, and there at the corner would be Ben, waiting in his car.

As Emily approached, Ben would leave his engine running and jump out to give her a big hug. He'd wrap his arms around her fluffy coat and squeeze her so tight that she'd let out a joyful squeak.

Ben took her to a new place every night: a bowling alley where everything was illuminated by black lights overhead so that whites and colors shone with an eerie luminescence; a pet store downtown where a horde of puppies slept peacefully in the front window; a hill overlooking the city that provided a perfect view of the local amusement park's weekly fireworks display.

They'd talk for hours about everything and nothing, and sometimes, staring at the city lights, they'd just sit together in silence as Emily wondered if they were thinking the same thoughts. Instead of discovering some unpleasant facts about him, Emily only liked him more and more with each date, until she felt her crush deepening into something more like love, though, of course, they were still a long way from saying that word out loud.

And every night, he'd get her home at midnight or two AM or later. He'd hug her good-bye, and she'd crawl into bed as her muscles ached and her mind drifted.

As the days passed, her lack of sleep started catching up to her, and Emily found her eyelids growing heavy in class. There just weren't enough hours in the day for school, swimming, and Ben, but which of the three was she supposed to give up?

She was asking herself just that question, shuffling down the hall one day after school, when she came around a corner and ran directly into Cameron Clark.

"Oh," he said. It was the first time she'd seen him look truly uncomfortable. "Hey."

"Cameron," she said. And then she drew a blank. What exactly *was* she supposed to say to her sister's ex?

"Listen, about the party," he said. "I shouldn't have mentioned your sister."

"No," she said. "It's okay. Samantha told me—"

"Samantha told you what?" he asked.

"That you and Sara, you know, dated."

Cameron snorted.

"I wish you were right," he said bitterly. "Sara and I—we trained together every day. Nobody pushed me like she did, and I think she would have said the same of me. She was one of—maybe *the* only girl at school I truly respected. Between sets, I used to tell her about all the girls I hooked up with. She'd just roll her eyes and give me a hard time." Cameron smiled slightly.

"I don't understand," said Emily.

"Sara…was amazing. A champion, a competitor. But, you know. She wasn't exactly popular. No one really thought she was hot. Except—I guess I did. I just didn't know it at the time, how much she meant to me."

His voice was shaking. He rubbed the bridge of his nose.

"I have these dreams where I go back—and instead of telling her about the other girls I dated, I ask her out instead. Maybe—maybe then things would have turned out differently—"

"But I heard she had a boyfriend."

"I've heard that rumor," said Cameron. "I told you before, though, Sara could definitely keep a secret. I told her everything. Yeah, everyone knows about the girls I've dated, but Sara actually knew about the ones who turned me down. She never told anyone. If she did have secrets of her own, she guarded them pretty close.... And if she had a boyfriend, he was a lucky guy."

Emily finished changing into her swimsuit before the next Thursday's practice. She was unsteady on her feet, and she had to brace herself against a locker as she straightened her swim cap.

"What's with the zombie impersonation?" asked Samantha from a few lockers over. "You do realize it's not Halloween, right?"

Emily hadn't seen Samantha alone since she'd gotten that ride home from Ben's party weeks ago, and since then, she'd been so focused on dating Ben that she hadn't really made an effort to track down Samantha. Now the older girl's words echoed in Emily's head.

"If your sister had time for a boyfriend, so do you."

But if Samantha hadn't been talking about Cameron, who could it be?

For a second, Emily paused. Maybe it was better if she didn't know. She'd always loved her sister, looked up to her. Knowing the truth could change everything.

"I'm just tired," Emily said.

"Well, get some sleep," said Samantha. "Quals for Junior Nationals are a week away. I'm not sure if it's your biggest priority anymore, but I'm pretty sure you don't want to lose to blondie."

Emily took a deep breath. She couldn't run away from the

truth. Even if what she found out about Sara wasn't pleasant, she had to know.

"Yeah," said Emily. "Hey, I've been meaning to ask.... You mentioned something about Sara—and a boyfriend?"

A shadow passed over Samantha's face.

"Look, I've tried to be nice to you about the whole thing," she said. "Out of respect, you know. She's gone now. Who cares what happened?"

She stripped off her sweater and tossed it violently into her locker.

"I do," said Emily.

Samantha started unlacing a big black combat boot. Her hands were tense and white against the laces.

"Nick and I—we were in love," said Samantha. "At least I thought we were. Then she came along and it was like he couldn't get rid of me fast enough."

"Nick?" asked Emily. "Nick Brown?" She felt her pulse pounding through her body, and her breathing quickened. Was it really possible?

"I know how much it hurt him to lose her," said Samantha. "But that doesn't make it any easier for me."

"I've—I've got to go," said Emily. She walked out of the locker room and out to the pool, where the shouts of the other swimmers echoed from every wall. Nick Brown—the same Nick Brown who had killed Sara—had been her *boyfriend*?

She leaned against the wall, trying not to pass out from the one-two punch of sleep deprivation and sheer emotional exhaustion.

144

"Kessler!" shouted her dad as he came up from behind her. "What's the holdup? Get into the pool!"

"Just a second."

"What's with the bags under your eyes?" he asked. "You having trouble sleeping? If you can't get to sleep, you're not training hard enough."

How much more could she take? Maybe this was the moment when she would break, when the weight of the sky became too much for her shoulders, and it crushed her beneath its weight.

She looked her dad—her coach—in the eyes. No, not yet. She wouldn't break. Not here, not now.

"I'm fine," Emily said, gritting her teeth.

Nick Brown, she thought, as if repeating the name inside her brain would force it to make sense. *Nick Brown. Nick Brown. Nick Brown.*

Then she walked to the side of the pool and jumped in.

"Kessler!" shouted Mr. McBride the next day in class.

"Huh?" asked Emily. "What?" She'd just been dreaming about sleeping on a very nice, very fluffy cloud next to Ben. Oh, no. She'd gotten to the point where she was literally dreaming about sleeping.

"I'm sorry," said Mr. McBride. "Did I wake you?"

"No. I was—concentrating."

Mr. McBride massaged his forehead, his fingers brushing against his bushy eyebrows.

"Well then," he said, "I'm sure you won't mind telling us

how the Hittites had such a profound combat advantage over their contemporaries."

"They, uh, developed bronze weapons?"

"Almost!" shouted Mr. McBride. "So very, very close! But in fact, the correct answer is that they were one of the first cultures to develop—wait for it—*iron* weapons, which cut through their enemies' bronze swords like a hot knife through butter." He put his hands on Emily's desk and looked down at her. "Minus one. And see me after class."

After class, Emily waited as the other students filtered out of the room, then calmly walked over to Mr. McBride's desk.

"About earlier," she said. "I'm sorry. I—"

"Not yet," he said, marking a large D-minus atop another student's essay. "We're expecting one more guest."

Confused, Emily turned to see Alicia Prez walk into the room.

"Ah, there she is," said Mr. McBride. "Please take a seat."

Alicia and Emily both sat down at desks near the front of the room.

"Just because I fell asleep once?" asked Emily. "How did you even have time to call her?"

"We were planning to meet with you already," he said, still not looking up from the paper. "Your little nap merely allowed me a chance to punctuate the statement we're about to make."

"I've been getting reports from a lot of your teachers that your performance is slipping in class," said Alicia. "Nothing too drastic—just a little drop from stellar down to above average. But what's got a lot of people worried is the way you look—it's like you can barely keep your eyes open."

"I haven't been getting much sleep lately," Emily confessed.

"Not too many students push themselves as hard as you do," said Alicia, scooting her desk closer to Emily. "There are plenty of students taking nothing but honors classes—and plenty more athletes—but to try to do both—"

"I'm doing fine," said Emily, standing up. She turned to Mr. McBride. "What's my grade in this class right now?"

He looked down at his notebook.

"B-minus."

She picked up her backpack, feeling her face glowing red with embarrassment.

"Fine," she said. "Then I'll just have to work harder."

"Emily," said Alicia, "that's not what we're trying to—"

But Emily didn't want to hear any more. It was just too much to take, especially from Alicia, who had been so proud of her before. She got up and left the room without another word.

"Hello?" called Kimi. "Earth to Emily! Are you ready?"

Emily sat on a bench outside the fitting rooms at the huge Macy's at the center of the mall as Kimi prepared to show her yet another dress. This would be the twelfth one she'd tried on, each more hideous than the last.

"Ready!" said Emily, trying not to let her exhaustion creep into her voice. As she and Kimi had scoured clothing racks in every corner of the mall, Emily realized two things: one, that she had never *really* gone dress shopping before, and two, that she didn't like it.

On each of her previous trips to the mall, Emily had come with her mom, or on infrequent, stressful occasions, her dad. She'd seen clothes as something functional—a way to ward off the cold and rain. She'd barely cared how she looked.

This was *real* dress shopping. Hitting every store at the mall with a girlfriend in tow, trying on any dress that looked even remotely flattering on the rack. By the time they'd been shopping for an hour, Emily's calves and feet ached, and she'd had to beg Kimi for a break so she could sit while Kimi tried on more dresses.

Still, shopping wasn't all bad. Normally Emily would have cringed at the thought of spending a Saturday afternoon this way, but given her current stress level, any distraction was a welcome one.

"What do you think?" asked Kimi as she emerged from the fitting room and twirled in a full-length green ball gown. This one hugged Kimi's body strangely, making her appear almost cylindrical instead of curvy.

"You look like a big cucumber," said Emily after a few seconds. "But maybe that's what you're going for?"

Kimi's face fell.

"That's not even attractive by vegetable standards."

She turned to go back to the dressing room.

"Whatever I end up getting, it has to be hotter than *any* possible dress Dominique and Lindsay could possibly find!" she shouted from behind the dressing-room door. "I need to look so good that *they* look like real estate agents in comparison!"

"Just don't overdo it," pleaded Emily. "Remember, it's homecoming, not prom. The ball gowns are just a little— much."

"This is impossible!" shouted Kimi, frustrated. "I may as well just go naked, like in my recurring nightmare."

"We'll find something—don't worry," said Emily, but her heart wasn't in it, and the words came out flat.

"So what's with you?" shouted Kimi. "Is everything okay?"

Everything most definitely *wasn't* okay. Emily had just found out her sister had been having a secret relationship with Nick Brown, her dad was getting suspicious about the bags under her eyes, and with Quals for Junior Nationals just around the corner, her muscles ached and she felt like she might pass out at any moment.

"Do you ever worry you don't really know the people in your life?" asked Emily. "Like, sure, you know the surface things about them. But deep down there's a whole other self you can never access."

"Definitely!" shouted Kimi. "Like on my dates with Phil, the guy could spend two hours talking about the new sound system his cousin just hooked up, with, like, sixteen different speakers positioned at precise angles to mimic true, movie-quality surround sound—but if I asked him what his relationship with his brother is like, he'd stare at me like I just burped or something."

"Yeah," said Emily. "That's—too bad." She loved Kimi, but the girl could be entirely dense sometimes. She hadn't even considered that Emily might have something important she wanted to talk about. Still, in a way, she appreciated Kimi's boy-crazy tirades; they were a nice change of pace from all the drama going on in Emily's own life.

Kimi emerged from the dressing room in a white shimmering dress that came down just over her knees. Cinched at the waist, it accentuated Kimi's natural curves. Emily couldn't believe it. Kimi didn't just look good. She looked like she'd walked in off the cover of *Cosmo*—or at least *Seventeen*.

"That's it," said Emily. "That's the one."

"I knew it!" said Kimi triumphantly. "That's why I saved it for last."

Thanks for that, thought Emily.

"Now it's your turn," said Kimi. "I've got a few ideas already!"

As they walked through the store, Emily pushed a cart that Kimi proceeded to drape with dresses as she updated Emily on her latest dating news.

"Okay, so, to recap. I broke the bad news to Phil on Wednesday. He took it well and said he still wanted to be friends, which, ironically, made him seem pretty sweet. I put it into his spreadsheet, and it gave him a nice little score boost—but not enough to make me regret dumping him."

"You do realize how crazy you sound, right?" asked Emily.

"Oh, definitely," said Kimi. "But I'm also the only girl at school *guaranteed* to have an amazing homecoming date. Present company excluded, of course."

"Thanks."

Kimi reached into a sale rack full of random dresses, pulled out a short burgundy one, and threw it onto the cart.

"How did you even see that?" asked Emily.

"I'm a shopping veteran," said Kimi. "Plus, my mom taught me everything she knows. I've got a sixth sense, a sales sense—kind of like Spidey sense. But for shopping. Swimming is your superpower. This is mine."

"So wait," said Emily. "If you and Phil broke up—"

"Right! I didn't finish telling you yet," said Kimi. "On Thursday, I caught Marcus at his locker and asked him if *he'd* like to go to homecoming. I talked about how sad I was about the breakup, and how he'd always seemed like a really sweet guy. He said he'd think about it, which basically means yes. Now I'm just waiting for him to call."

She pulled another dress off the rack and threw it in the cart.

"Okay," she said. "I think that's enough to get you started."

Half an hour later, Emily stood in the dressing room, checking out a long, black sequined gown that Kimi had tossed over the door to her. It sparkled in the overhead lights, even more so when she moved. She turned her body to check herself out in profile. She had to admit, she looked hot. After six hideous, over-the-top dresses that Kimi had gushed over but Emily had loathed, maybe this was the one.

"Okay, Kimi," she called. "I'm coming out!"

She opened the door, walked outside, and raised her arms.

"Ta-da!" she said. She had to admit, she was actually starting to have fun.

"Oooh," said Kimi. "Very femme fatale. I could totally picture you slipping some poison into James Bond's drink."

"Is that a good thing?"

"It's definitely hot," said Kimi, who had gotten up from the bench and was circling Emily to check her out from multiple angles. "I'm just not sure if it's *you*."

"Please don't tell me I have to try on another dress." Emily's patience was nearly exhausted.

"Just one more!" insisted Kimi. "Please, please, please! I think I saw a really good one over on a thirty percent off rack! Go start changing, and I'll get it for you."

As Emily sadly walked back into the dressing room and stripped off the black dress, she thought about all of the other things she could be doing with this time: homework, laps, sleeping. That last one sounded pretty nice. She sat on the small seat in the corner of the dressing room and closed her eyes, feeling on the edge of dozing off.

So it was no coincidence that the blue dress's appearance felt like something out of a dream. Emily opened her eyes to see the shimmering blue fabric sailing over the fitting-room door. It looked almost like a splash of water flying through the air, as if Kimi had tossed a bucketful of it at Emily. But the dress that landed in her arms was indeed real and dry. Seeing it, she felt as she had when she first saw Ben Kale: that it was made for her.

Even before she tried it on, even before she walked out and saw Kimi's eyes go wide, Emily knew: She had found her dress.

At ten twenty-five that night, Emily stood in front of her closet mirror, holding the dress up to her body and examining it in the light. She imagined Ben looking at her, a big, surprised smile on his face. *"You look so beautiful,"* said the fantasy Ben. *"I'd give anything to kiss a girl as pretty as you."*

She pursed her lips and half contemplated wearing it tonight, before she opened the window and felt the harsh autumn cold blow across her skin. She laid the dress out across her bed and put on her thickest coat. Better to surprise Ben at the dance anyway. A text appeared on her phone: *Rdy when u r.* ☺

A few minutes later, Emily walked toward Ben's car. Her head felt like it was full of helium, and as she floated across the sidewalk, she stumbled from time to time. Had she ever been this tired in her life? She had passed the point of mere exhaustion and entered a state of blissful sleep deprivation where everything seemed hilarious. She hoped she wasn't going crazy.

As she approached Ben, he took her in his arms and spun her around, and a warm spark of happiness filled her chest.

In these moments, when she was wrapped up in his arms, she knew that the lack of sleep and constant fear of getting caught were worth it. Because nothing else in her life made her feel like this, not swimming, not even winning races.

"What's gotten into you?" asked Ben. "You're, uh, holding me kind of tight."

"Just don't let go of me," she said. "I'm worried I'll float away."

And he held her tight until she felt gravity return to normal.

After their usual coffee, he took her to the beach that night. The tide was low and, flashlight in hand, he led her down to look at starfish and sea urchins clinging to rocks in tide pools.

"Here," he said. "Run your fingers along that one's back. It feels like sandpaper. Oh, don't touch that one, though. That one's poisonous."

She drew back her hand and looked at him suspiciously.

"How many girlfriends have you gotten killed on dates like this?"

Ben started counting on his fingers, as if trying to add them all up.

"Come on," she said, drying her hand off on his T-shirt. "What else have you got to show me?"

"Believe me," he said. "I'm just getting started."

They followed the rocky coastline down toward a barren cliff face, and Ben shone his flashlight's beam into a cave's black mouth.

"There it is," he said. "No one outside of my family seems to know about this place."

"Is it safe?" asked Emily.

Ben shrugged.

"Seriously," she said. "I'm not kidding."

"I won't let anything happen to you. You trust me?"

"I trust you." She took his hand and followed him into the dark. After they'd walked a few steps in, Ben turned off his flashlight.

"What are you doing?" she asked.

"Just walk where I walk. You'll understand in a minute."

As they went deeper into the cave, Emily's pulse quickened. How well did she even know Ben? What if he was just leading her toward some bottomless pit that he'd push her into? She imagined falling forever, knowing the boy she'd loved had betrayed her. Or what if he'd decided he couldn't wait for that kiss any longer and was planning to do it here in the dark. Or what if—

"Okay," he said. "We're here. Count to three."

"Three?" she asked.

"Two," he said. "One."

He flicked on his flashlight, and the beam shot straight up, illuminating a glittering ceiling of pure amethyst. The purple crystals shot refracted light around the chamber, revealing still more of their glittering cousins.

"It's—amazing," said Emily.

Ben held her hands in his. Then he leaned in and kissed her softly on the cheek.

"I've never brought a girl here."

"Ben—I don't know what to say."

"You like it?"

She leaned in, kissed him back on the cheek, and smiled.

"I love it."

She had no idea how long they stood there, under the purple light of the amethysts. She knew only that after a while her knees felt stiff and her face grew cold. By the time they got back out, and Emily thought to check the time on her phone, she realized it was 3 AM.

"I'm never going to catch up on sleep," she said.

"Oh," said Ben. "I'm sorry. I really am. I forget about your schedule sometimes. Well, maybe I forget on purpose."

"Don't apologize," said Emily. "This was amazing. You're amazing. I wouldn't have traded this for a week's worth of sleep."

As it turned out, the amethyst cave wasn't Ben's final surprise of the night. When they reached Emily's block and Ben put the car in park, he told Emily he had a present for her.

"Open the glove compartment," he said.

When she did, Emily found a long box wrapped in silver paper, the kind that might house a necklace or a watch. As she carefully unstuck the tape at one end and slipped a wooden box out of the wrapping paper, she wondered what it could be. It felt too light to be jewelry.

"I just want you to know," said Ben, "that I wouldn't have gotten this for anyone but you."

She opened the box to find…

"A piece of paper!" she said. "Just what I've always wanted."

"Unfold it."

The paper was a progress report from that day at 3 PM. It listed each of Ben's classes, along with his current grades.

AP Calculus	A
AP English Literature	A-
Health	A
AP Physics	A
Gym	B+
AP Government	A

"Wait a second," she said. "Did you hack the school computer system or something?"

He smiled.

"Not this time. I actually studied. These grades are for real."

Now it was Emily's turn to smile.

"You're only getting a B-plus in gym?" she asked.

"I know, I know. I promised I'd get my grades up. But I don't do laps, Em. I just don't."

"So this means—" she started.

"That I'm allowed to participate in school activities again," he said. "You've got yourself a homecoming date."

As Ben pulled away and Emily walked home, she danced a few steps, pirouetted, and bowed to the street. She was officially going to homecoming with Ben Kale. No matter how tired she was, no matter what happened now, nothing could take that away.

The huge smile on her face quickly fell, though, as she approached her house to find the lights on, including the one in her bedroom. A sick feeling entered her stomach. *No*, she thought. *No. No. No.*

She opened her window from the outside, like usual, then climbed up onto the sill and hefted her body over the ledge. Inside, though, she didn't find her bedroom's usual welcoming darkness. Instead, she found her parents. She fell in a heap inside at the foot of the window and looked up at her father. He shook with anger.

"Welcome back," he said. "We've got a lot to talk about."

CHAPTER ELEVEN

"What are you doing in here?" asked Emily as she got to her feet. She rubbed her tailbone, hoping she hadn't bruised it.

"What were *you* doing *not* in here is the better question," her dad shouted. "Not that you have to answer. I received an anonymous e-mail earlier today informing me that you've been sneaking out at night to see a boy. I didn't want to believe it. Now I have no choice."

Emily didn't have to think too hard to guess the e-mail's writer. *Dominique.*

"I was just, uh, training."

"Training?" her father asked. "Training?! Do you have any idea how much you've probably damaged your swimming career? Who even *knows* how many hours of sleep debt you've accumulated. It could take months to undo the physical strain you've put on your body—and Quals are coming up on Thursday!"

Meanwhile, Emily's mother said nothing and looked worriedly back and forth between Emily and her husband. In a way, Emily wished she would say something—the guilty knowledge that she'd made her mom stay up worrying was already starting to gnaw at her. She must have been waiting for hours.

"Well?!" Emily's dad shouted. "What have you got to say for yourself?"

"Dad, don't—"

"Call me Coach!"

"But we're at home." Emily was shocked. She'd rarely seen her father get this angry.

"I don't care where we are!"

"Paul," said Emily's mom, "you need to calm down."

"This is between me and my athlete," said Emily's dad, turning to her.

"This is between us and our daughter."

"No," said Emily, sniffling. "He's right. This is between us, Mom. Give us a minute." Her dad's anger she could deal with, but Emily just couldn't handle the worried look on her mom's face right now.

"Fine," said Emily's mom as she turned and left. "Fine."

As soon as she was gone, Emily's father returned to his tirade.

"The idea that you'd throw away everything I've worked for, all for some idiotic, schoolgirl crush—"

Emily wanted to scream at the unfairness of it all. Ben was more than just a crush, and what did her father mean by "everything *I've* worked for"? But what was the point in speaking up? It wasn't like he would listen.

"Starting tomorrow," he said, "you're telling that boy it's over. I'll be up all night, figuring out a new schedule for you, and maybe, just maybe, I can get you in good enough shape to make it through Thursday's Quals."

"Please," she said, and she felt hot tears beginning to swell under her eyelids. "Please—"

"Give me your phone," he said, and Emily, scanning the room, realized he'd already taken her computer. Once the phone was gone, her last link to the outside world would be gone. "Now."

She dug her cell out of her jeans pocket and handed it to him. After he'd scanned her last few texts, Emily's father shook his head disgustedly and slipped the phone into his pocket. She wondered if she'd ever see it again. Then he turned, slamming the door behind him. Emily sat on her bed and brought her knees to her chest. It wasn't until then that she remembered the blue homecoming dress. She'd left it right there on the bed. Now it was gone.

She leaped up and frantically searched the far side of the bed, hoping against hope that it had fallen into the crack between the mattress and the wall. No luck. She pulled off the sheets and quilt. Still nothing. She riffled through her closet—maybe her mother had hung it up. She flipped through the clothes, hoping to toss aside her ugly T-shirts and come up with a handful of soft blue fabric.

No. No. No!

She reached the end of the closet, turned back, and searched the rest of the room one more time before she finally gave up and collapsed into a ball on her barren mattress. In her gut, she already knew it: Her father had taken the dress.

Ancient religions had predicted an apocalypse in 1000 AD. Scientists had warned of massive computer malfunctions in Y2K. Others predicted that the end of the world would come in 2012. For Emily Kessler, the world ended one cold November day.

At least, that's what it felt like.

The apocalypse began before the first bell even rang. Emily opened her locker, found a bouquet of roses, and turned around to find Ben smiling at her.

"Don't look so surprised," he said. "Compared to hacking the school's computers to switch that newspaper headline, figuring out your locker combination was easy. I was worried when I didn't hear from you Sunday, so I decided to—"

"It's very sweet," she said. "But—"

"But you're allergic to roses?"

"No."

"But the color red fills you with inexplicable, boiling rage?"

Why did he have to make this so impossible?

"But I can't go to the dance with you."

Now it was Ben's turn to be surprised.

"You can't—what?"

"Saturday night when I got home—my dad was waiting up for me."

"He knows?"

"Everything."

"Okay," he said, still smiling. "This is okay. We'll deal with this. Sneaking around is going to be a little tougher, but I've always managed before."

"Ben," she said. "No."

"We'll make it work. You'll see. We'll come up with something. I *know* we can figure out some 'class assignment' for you to do the night of homecoming. I can probably even get you a teacher's note or something. And then for our weekday dates, we can just play it by ear."

She shook her head. "You don't get it. It's too hard, Ben. I can't go on like this. Look at me, I'm a wreck. I can't be with you and still be the person I want to be."

A small crowd of students was starting to gather as they talked. They watched Emily and Ben and whispered to one another.

"So that's it?" asked Ben.

"I know I messed up. You worked so hard the last couple of weeks catching up on homework and studying for tests so you could take me to this stupid dance—"

"It's not stupid," he said. "I don't know why I ever said that. The truth is, I really want to take you."

"Ben, you don't understand. I can't."

"You won't even *try* to go with me?"

"I'm sorry," said Emily, crying softly now. "I never meant to hurt you."

"Forget it," said Ben, looking sadder than she'd ever seen him. "I never thought you were the type of person to give up so easily. I guess I was wrong about you."

As he turned and walked away, Emily stood there stupidly clutching the roses that only a few minutes ago he'd been so happy to give her. Now he'd never give her flowers again.

She looked around to see a dozen sets of eyes watching her.

"What?!" she shouted. "Show's over! Go tell your friends!"

She shoved the bouquet into a nearby trash can, but it wouldn't quite go down. She pushed harder and harder, grinding the flowers until a knot of stems and petals protruded from the lid. The roses were a mangled mess, and she looked at them, thinking, *That, right there, is my life.*

Then she walked to her locker, slammed it shut, and headed off to class.

At lunch, things got worse. As Emily settled into her usual spot at the center table, Hannah Carmichael leaned over and whispered, "No offense, sweetie, but you might not want to sit here today."

Emily was almost too dazed to respond. All she could muster was a confused "Huh?"

"Word is out," said Hannah. "Everyone knows how you

totally broke Ben's heart. Now, I'm not as judgmental as, you know, *certain people* at this school, but still, he'll be showing up any second, and you might want to do him the courtesy of giving him a little space."

"Yeah," said Emily, picking up her cup of yogurt from the table. "Sure."

She walked away from the table and off toward the far corner of the cafeteria, only to find Dominique sitting there, listening to her huge headphones and reciting some sort of mantra. Great. Emily couldn't even go back to her old spot.

As Emily passed by, Dominique broke from her trance, smiled, and said, "You look a little upset, Em. I hope your dad didn't get any incriminating e-mails or anything."

"You could have done this anytime you wanted," said Emily. "Why now?"

"It just seemed like the right time," said Dominique. "But don't worry. You're tough. I'm sure you'll still be ready for Quals on Thursday, no matter what else happens to be going on in your personal life. I just hope it doesn't affect your grades. I mean, I hear McBride's tough. Is it true he docks you a full letter if you lose your history textbook?"

A sudden sinking feeling entered Emily's chest. She opened her backpack to look at her textbooks. There was English...Biology...

But no History. The book was gone.

"You should really be more careful about leaving your valuables in the locker room," added Dominique. "Things get stolen all the time."

"You're a b—" Emily looked over her shoulder to see if any teachers were around to hear her swear. One was. "A bad person."

Dominique shrugged.

"I do whatever it takes to win. You taught me that. See you at the races, Swimbot."

Emily briefly contemplated starting a nail-scratching, hair-pulling, old-fashioned girl fight. It *would* feel nice to mess up Dominique's pretty little face. But there was too much to lose. A fight might put their eligibility to swim on Thursday at risk. Better just to beat Dominique in the pool. If Emily *could* beat Dominique.

Emily turned away without another word and pushed through the door that led to the school's exterior courtyard. Outside, the sun shone through wispy clouds. It was the kind of day that *looked* warm but actually felt so bitterly cold you needed a sweater under your jacket to keep from shivering. All Emily had on was an old hoodie of Sara's.

She crouched down and rested against the cafeteria wall and ate her lunch with shaking hands. It was all over now— Ben, her new supposed "friends," all of it. Dominique had the right idea: Emily would be Swimbot again.

She felt herself rocking and wondered if she might just pitch forward. Weren't there old monks somewhere who picked a tree to sit under and waited around until they either reached enlightenment or starved to death? Maybe she could just sit here like that.

"Hey."

Emily turned her head a little to the side and saw Kimi settling in beside her.

"Thanks for coming out," said Emily softly. "But I'd kind of rather be alone."

Kimi sighed, her long gray dress and black boots mirroring the day's dreary mood.

"Don't think I'm coming out only for you," she said. "I'm not exactly welcome at the center table anymore, either."

"Yeah?"

"Let's just say I may have miscalculated when I thought I could dump Phil for Marcus. Apparently, contrary to what popular culture would have you believe, boys sometimes *do* talk to each other about relationships."

"Sorry."

"It gets worse," said Kimi. "I *kind of* accidentally left a few documents open in my e-mail on a library computer. And Amir *kind of* forwarded them to his account so he could study them in depth. And he may have *kind of* mass-forwarded them to everyone at school."

"So all those pro/con sheets you made—"

"Public knowledge. What guy in school is going to *ever* want to go to a dance with me now?"

"Wow. So someone's life *does* suck worse than mine."

"Thanks. That's nice. Really."

"Sorry if I'm not exactly in the mood to comfort you about your boy drama."

"Well, I'm sorry if my life isn't as tragic as yours," said Kimi, getting to her feet. "Sorry for bothering you with my stupid little problems."

"Kimi, I didn't mean—"

"Even when our lives are going *well* you find a way to make me feel bad about things. Why would I *possibly* think you could console me now?"

"Kimi," Emily started. "Wait. I didn't mean to—" But it was too late. Emily's best friend—the only friend she had left—was gone.

At the point when her friendship with Kimi imploded, Emily was pretty sure her day couldn't get any worse. She was wrong. By the time she arrived at Honors History, Emily was so upset about her talk with Kimi that she'd completely forgotten about her missing textbook—that is, until Mr. McBride shouted, "Books out! Flip to two-thirty-nine to consult table twenty-two B. Chinese dynasties."

Emily unzipped her backpack and looked helplessly inside, willing her textbook to reappear. It did not.

"Ms. Kessler," Mr. McBride said, stopping by her desk. "Left our book at home, did we?"

"No," she said quietly. She thought about trying to explain what Dominique had done, but it seemed pointless. She had no proof, and Mr. McBride wasn't the type to believe students' excuses anyway.

"Oh?" he asked. "You're not trying to tell me it's—"

"It's lost," she said, defeated, trying not to let her face

betray any emotion. Her B-minus would become a C-minus now, the lowest grade she'd ever gotten.

Mr. McBride took a step back and looked away from her.

"Right," he said. "Most unfortunate. You'll have to look on with another student for the time being. Please come see me after class if you'd like to discuss your other options."

When class ended, though, Emily just couldn't face him. She picked up her backpack and left without a word.

For the next three nights, Emily could have gone to sleep at ten thirty like usual. She was certainly in bed by then, earlier even. Trying to make up for her lost hours of rest, her dad had instituted a nine o'clock bedtime. But instead of sleeping, Emily stared at the ceiling, thinking about everything that had gone wrong. Ben seemed to have disappeared off the face of the earth, Kimi wasn't speaking to her, and Emily couldn't even get online to IM Kimi, since her dad had taken the computer.

If Sara really had dated Nick Brown, Emily was starting to understand why she'd kept it a secret. As it turned out, the truth often had consequences—especially when their dad was involved.

Emily's mind ran in loops as she tried to figure out how everything had gone wrong, and whether it could be fixed, but no matter how many times she thought things through, the solution eluded her. She might as well have tried to stick a broken egg back together with glue and tape. She couldn't sneak out anymore, and there was certainly no way she could go to the dance. And she was who she was. She couldn't change into the kind of friend Kimi wanted her to be.

Over and over again, she imagined Ben showing up at an unfamiliar house in a well-tailored suit. He approached the doorway and pulled a bouquet of roses from behind his back as Lindsay or Hannah or even Kimi opened the door. The girl threw her arms around him and nearly devoured him with kisses before tossing the flowers carelessly aside and running with him hand in hand to his car. After they'd left, Emily, who had been watching from behind a tree, would pick up the flowers to smell them, but they'd turn stale and brittle at her touch, collapsing into dust.

Ben wasn't hers anymore. He could do what he wanted— and he could have any girl he wanted. It was only a matter of time before her fantasy would become reality and the final, intact piece of her heart would break for good.

It was all gone. All of it. The only course of action seemed clear. She would resign herself to misery, just like she had before the year started. There was only one thing left: winning.

CHAPTER
TWELVE

Quals for Junior Nationals took place at Spartan Academy, an all-boys prep school thirty minutes from Twin Branches that boasted the best swimming facilities in the state. Modeled on prestigious East Coast prep schools, Spartan Academy was built of imported red brick covered with ivy. Everything about it seemed expensive and old.

The swimming facilities themselves, however, were brand-new and state-of-the-art. Four Olympic-size pools sat side by side, all housed within an enormous glass shell that included a retractable roof and walls for warmer seasons.

As the Twin Branches swim team entered the building, Emily looked across the room to see a half dozen other squads stretching and gossiping. Many of the girls pointed to her and Dominique, the clear favorites.

Quals was composed of several heats for each stroke and distance, with eight swimmers participating in every round. The top two finishers from each race would then advance to the finals, and the top two from *those* races would receive invitations to the Junior Nationals in two weeks. If all went as planned, Dominique and Emily would represent California in most of those races.

That wasn't to say that there wouldn't be competition. Girls like Mira Syzbalski from Monarch Prep, who, aptly, specialized in butterfly, stood a chance of unseating them in a given race. If they wanted to qualify, Dominique and Emily would need to bring their A games.

And right now, Emily was about as far off her game as she could get. Raccoon-eyed from lack of sleep, she could barely walk a straight line much less swim one.

Her first race was the 50-meter freestyle, thankfully a short event that she excelled in. Even better, Dominique had been placed in a different heat. They wouldn't see each other until the finals, provided they both got there.

As Emily got up on her block, her father, dressed in his usual gray suit, approached and looked up and down the lanes.

"No one you really need to worry about in this heat," he said. "Julia Weiss over in lane three has posted a few decent times, but nothing close to yours, and there are a couple of girls I've never seen swim, but we would have heard about it if anyone was close to your level."

Emily nodded, and without a word to her dad, she adjusted her position on the block. For the first time she could remember, though, the grain of the plastic against her feet felt unfamiliar, and the world seemed to pulse with light. She knelt down and stood up, trying to loosen her muscles, but instead she felt a strange rushing sensation, as if all the blood had suddenly drained from her.

"Hey," said the girl from the next lane over. "Are you okay?"

It was the last thing Emily heard before she fell forward into the pool.

The next thing Emily knew, she was underwater. She looked up to see the other girls staring down at her. Maybe it would be better just to stay here—at least that way she could avoid the embarrassment of facing them. Was there anyone above the water who even cared if she swam back up?

She floated there, motionless, weighing her options—and then someone splashed down into the water, wrapped his arms around her, and dragged her to the surface. It wasn't until he'd pulled her up to the edge of the pool that she realized it was her father.

"Are you okay?" he asked.

"Yeah. I must have—slipped."

His gray suit had gone black with the wet. He looked less intimidating now, with his suit soaked and clinging to his puffy body—like an overgrown child wearing his father's clothes. He emptied his pockets to reveal a soaked wallet and a shorted-out cell.

"You could have—" He looked around him at the

gathering crowd of concerned swimmers and parents. He straightened his wet tie. "You could have been disqualified! A few seconds later, and the judges would have counted that as a false start."

So that was it. For a few seconds, Emily had seen true fear in her father's eyes—fear that he'd lose another daughter. She'd wanted so badly to reach up and hug him, to thank him for jumping in and saving her. And then her dad had disappeared, replaced by her *coach*.

As Emily got up and walked back toward her starting block, the crowd gave a small round of applause, glad to see she wasn't seriously hurt. The only one who didn't clap was Dominique, who stood watching Emily with her arms folded and a look of pure contempt on her face.

Emily walked back to her block and got on top of it, steady this time. The world seemed in better focus now. As much as her dad pushed her—as much as he made her life miserable—he had jumped into the pool to pull her out when no one else would. That was worth something, right? For the first time in several dark days, she saw a glimmer of light.

Maybe she could do it. Maybe she did have it in her. She wasn't at full strength—that much was obvious—but maybe she'd still swim well enough to beat these girls.

A minute later, the horn blew, and the race began. The first twenty-five meters went by like normal, but Emily knew something was wrong as she touched the far wall. Her muscles had already begun to scream, something that didn't usually happen in a race this short.

She tried to ignore the pain and keep up her usual pace, but it was no use. It felt like she was swimming through oatmeal instead of water, like every stroke might rip her muscles from her bones or her arms from her body.

She touched the far wall and looked up at the huge timer on the opposite wall. She was a full second and a half over her usual time, a huge margin in a race this short. In the next lane over, two unfamiliar girls cheered and embraced as Emily realized that they, not she, had qualified for the finals.

The rest of the day went only slightly better. Emily reached the finals for about half of the events, though she didn't qualify in *every* stroke, as her father had expected her to. Dominique, on the other hand, dominated her heats, outdistancing her competitors by several body-lengths or more in nearly every race.

"Rough day, Em," said Dominique. "Did you notice I set a new personal record in fifty-meter backstroke, by the way? Twenty-eight-point-nine seconds."

"The only records you'll ever set are personal," said Emily, gesturing to the large electronic board on the wall, where the scores and names of national record holders in each event were illuminated. Near the bottom, it blinked out:

SARA KESSLER, 50M BACKSTROKE, 28.3

Dominique glanced at the board and shrugged. "We'll see."

* * *

Emily and Dominique faced off in a dozen races during the qualifying rounds to see who went to Nationals. Dominique won all twelve. No matter how hard Emily willed her body forward, she just couldn't seem to catch up to her rival, whose movements through the water seemed unjustly effortless.

Luckily, Emily managed to place second in several of the races. Though she hadn't won today, she'd at least get an invitation to the Junior Nationals, where possible redemption awaited.

Yet when she looked at the times Dominique was posting, Emily's heart sank. Even at her best, Emily had never swum that fast. Now that Dominique had fully dedicated herself to winning, she was better than ever. Maybe unbeatable.

As they prepared for their last race of the day, the 50-meter backstroke, Dominique leaned over into Emily's lane and whispered, "Good luck out there. I just *know* you're due to win at least *one* race today!"

Emily felt a surge of angry adrenaline course through her veins. Good. Maybe it would help her win. She reached up from the pool and grabbed the underside of the block, getting into start position for backstroke.

When the gun went off, she pushed off hard, and for the first time that day, Emily didn't feel tired. Maybe it was the adrenaline, or maybe she'd passed the point of exhaustion to where she couldn't even feel anything. In either case, the pool seemed to part a little more easily, and she skimmed across the lane like a water strider. She made a good turn at the far wall and barreled back, looking for the flags overhead. Finally, she felt her fingers touch the far wall and heard the crowd explode in applause.

She pulled off her goggles and looked up at the leaderboard. The first thing she saw was her time:

EMILY KESSLER, 50M BACKSTROKE, 28.7

She could hardly believe it. After the day she'd had, everything she'd gone through, she'd set a new personal record—a time that was only a few milliseconds behind Sara's national record. Her heart leaped.

And then it burst, as if shot down by some malicious hunter. Right above her name was Dominique's. She'd swum the race in twenty-eight seconds. Flat.

Not only had Dominique beaten Emily, she'd beaten Sara.

It was a long drive home. At first, Emily's father could barely look at her. Finally, he said, "I thought you'd be the one winning every race. You were so dedicated. You could have had it all. Now I see I should have been putting more time into Dominique all along."

"Looks like it."

"Sara—" he said. "Sara would never have lost like that."

"Well, it looks like even Sara wasn't good enough today."

There was a new record holder in the 50-meter backstroke. Sara's name would be crossed out of the record books, replaced by Dominique's.

"Yes," her father said, rubbing at the bridge of his nose. "I guess you're right." He gripped the wheel hard, and Emily was thankful her mom had skipped this meet—her mom always worked herself up into such a state, worrying he'd give himself a heart attack as he drove.

"One more thing," he added. "You may have noticed that the Junior Nationals falls on the same weekend as that homecoming dance you were planning to attend. Just in case you had any idea of sneaking out again, I pulled some strings and made sure that all of your heats are scheduled for the Saturday-night block."

Heats for the various matches took place all day Saturday and Sunday, and the organizers could have scheduled her for any block of time. But her dad asked them to choose that one. Just to let her know *he* was in charge of her life. She would have cried, but she was just too tired, too beaten down to even react. She let herself sag against the side of the car and felt the cold of the window glass against her cheek as her last hopes of going to homecoming died.

They drove the rest of the way home in total silence.

The next Monday at school, Emily ate her lunch as fast as possible outside the cafeteria, then ran straight for the library, where no one would bother her. At least it was warm there. She logged on to one of the computers to check her e-mail and Facebook for the first time in days and found an invitation to a group called I Bet I Can Find 500 Twin Branches Students Who Don't Like Kimi Chen. Curious, she clicked the link.

She found a page featuring a picture of Kimi with devil horns Photoshopped onto her forehead and a wall of posts, most of which were by angry guys upset about the ratings Kimi had given them. Several had written their own pro/con sheets about Kimi, none of which were very nice.

Con: I dress like a schizophrenic clown.
Con: I'm actually kind of ugly.
Con: No one likes me.

Emily closed the window. Suddenly, Kimi's problems didn't seem so trivial, and Emily felt a strange mixture of guilt and anger. Yeah, Kimi had messed up, but this was way worse than she deserved. And worst of all, Emily wasn't even there to comfort her. Some friend she'd turned out to be.

By the time the end of the day arrived, Emily's father had already printed out a new placard and placed it on the Twin Branches High leaderboard on the wall above the pool. It read:

DOMINIQUE CLARK, 50M BACKSTROKE, 28.0

Emily stood looking at it as she waited for her father to show up for her individual coaching session.

When fifteen minutes passed and he still hadn't shown, she walked down to the counselor's office and asked if she could use the phone. She dialed her dad's cell before remembering that he'd destroyed it jumping into the pool to save her. She decided to try the home phone.

"Hello?" he answered.

"Dad, what's going on? I'm here waiting for you."

"I figured if neither of us wanted to be there, what's the point," he said at the other end of the line.

"Dad, don't do this."

"Why should I keep trying when you won't?"

"Please, please don't give up on me."

"Em, you already gave up on yourself."

He hung up without saying good-bye.

For a while, Emily just sat in the empty counselor's office, looking at the keypad, wondering if there was anyone she could possibly call. She didn't even know Kimi's number—she'd always counted on her cell to remember it for her. She was half contemplating dialing up a random stranger to talk to when she felt a tap on her shoulder and looked around to see Alicia.

"Emily, how nice to bump into you. I've been looking for you, actually."

Emily wiped at her eyes, hoping she wasn't tearing up.

"Everything okay?" Alicia asked. "You want to talk about it?"

"Not really."

Alicia sat down on a chair in the counselor's waiting room and gestured for Emily to sit with her. She reluctantly complied.

"Look, I'm not going to be one of those adults who comes in and tries to tell you your problems are small, or that they'll go away, or that I can solve them for you," said Alicia. "Honestly, for me at least, high school was the most stressful time of my life. Way worse than college. And I'm sure I didn't even have to deal with half of what you're going through. I was just a straight-up nerd. I didn't play sports. And I never had to deal with some other girl stealing one of my textbooks."

"You heard about that?"

"Just a rumor in the faculty lunchroom—not enough to actually punish anyone, but I'm tempted to believe it." Alicia opened her bag and pulled out a book. It took a few seconds for Emily to realize it was a history textbook.

"Would you believe that Honors History was my favorite class back when Mr. McBride was *my* teacher?" asked Alicia. "Or that I loved it so much I 'lost' my textbook on purpose? Of course, those were in the days before he started docking you a letter grade for that. I just had to pay a twenty-dollar replacement fee."

She handed the book over to Emily.

"I wish I could do more," she said. "I know you're going through a lot. But maybe the book will help just a little."

For a few seconds, Emily just sat there, dazed, looking at the textbook, not knowing what to say. Finally she asked, "You were a nerd?"

Alicia smiled. "Definitely. Still am. What other twenty-three-year-old would be so eager to go back to high school?"

Emily took the book and tucked it under her arm.

"Thanks," she said. "This really helps."

"The rest is up to you," said Alicia. "Good luck. As hopeless as things seem, remember, they will get better."

A few minutes later, after Alicia had left, Emily walked back to the pool. She sat by the edge of the pool and dangled her feet over the side, feeling the warm water against her toes. She looked again at the leaderboard, where her sister's name had now been replaced by Dominique's.

Things had seemed better after her talk with Alicia, but seeing the changed leaderboard brought her feeling of helplessness flooding back. Maybe her father was right. What was the point of going on if no matter how well you swam, someone would eventually come along and erase your name? Sara had given everything to swimming, and what had it given her in return? A name on a leaderboard that was destined to be replaced.

Emily must have been sitting alone with her thoughts for twenty minutes before he came in. She recognized the long shadow, the figure distorted by a camera that hung around his neck.

"I had to see it to believe it," said Nick Brown. "I thought her name would be up there forever—or at least for a few more years."

She was too tired to scream at him this time. Instead, she spoke with soft, slow-boiling rage.

"Someone like you could never know what it means to have your name up on that board." She refused to look at him.

"What's that supposed to mean?"

"She gave up everything—everything—to get her name on that board. And then you—you took it all away."

"I'm sorry," he said. "I really am. I loved her, too, you know."

She turned to look at him now and saw that he was crying. He wasn't sobbing, but tears were unmistakably rolling down his face. She wasn't sure she'd ever seen a guy her age cry like that, even an emo one like Nick Brown. Was what Samantha had said true? Could Nick and Sara really have dated?

Hot tears escaped her eyes. Sara was erased now, forever. And even worse, the sister she'd known had apparently been a fake. If she and Nick had really dated, then Sara had spent the last year of her life lying to Emily.

"I don't even—" Emily said. "I don't even know who she was."

Nick knelt by her side and offered her a packet of tissues from his backpack.

"I do," he said. "Will you come with me for a minute?"

"Come with you?" she asked, getting to her feet. "Whatever happened, whoever you were to her—it doesn't change the fact that you killed her."

She imagined throwing him in the pool, jumping in after him, and forcing him to the bottom. She imagined keeping him there until he took a deep lungful of water.

Nick looked stricken, but Emily kept talking. "You put her in your car and drove off the road and killed her."

"Emily," he said. "I wasn't driving."

CHAPTER
THIRTEEN

The yearbook room glowed with the faint blue light of computer monitors and smelled like rotten eggs, and Emily, despite being used to the constant scent of chlorine, made a face as she walked in.

"Sorry about that," said Nick. "We still have a traditional photo-processing lab in back, and the chemicals kind of stink."

"What are we doing here?"

"I've got all my photos from the last year stored here. I figured if you really wanted to get to know your sister, this would be a good place to start."

He booted up the computer and clicked through a few files before getting to one called Summer/Fall/Winter Sara Photos.

"These pictures didn't exactly make it into the yearbook," said Nick, his finger hovering over the mouse, ready to click open the folder. "Sara made a big deal over keeping our relationship a secret. Almost no one at school knew about it. Then after she was—gone—she kind of became this legend, you know? The girl who'd given up everything for her swimming. Most people didn't know she even had a social life. And when I saw your dad in the ER the night she died, he wouldn't even let me go into her room. I tried calling him a couple of days later, to see if I could come to the funeral, but he wouldn't talk to me other than to say I'd better stay away. I think he preferred to pretend that I didn't exist, that I was just some stranger. Maybe she and I—our relationship—didn't fit with the image of the perfect daughter he had in his head."

Emily sat glassy-eyed, trying to take it all in. Her father had known about Nick and Sara?

"You said you weren't driving," she said, remembering why she'd come here in the first place. "Who was?"

"I was teaching her. We'd been practicing for weeks. When she was supposed to do her jog home, I'd get in the passenger seat, and she'd get behind the wheel. Your dad wouldn't give her lessons. He said it would be too dangerous. Really, though, I think he didn't want her to be able to go where she wanted. He didn't want to give up that control."

"Sara was driving?"

"She begged me to teach her," he said. "She'd never driven in the rain before. It was late and wet, the first storm of the season. Before sunset, I'd been leaning out the window, taking photos of the clouds as your sister drove. And then it was dark. Time to go home. Except we didn't make it back to your place. We came around a bend—not even going fast or anything—and the car just kept skidding on a patch of water. Right over the side of a ditch."

"My dad—he never told me. He always said that you—"

"What's it matter?" Nick asked. "It's still my fault. Even if I wasn't behind the wheel, I was still the one who let her drive. Everyone just assumed I was the driver—and I felt so guilty about what happened—I let them think what they wanted. We'd always kept each other's secrets. I wanted to keep this last one."

Emily turned back to look at the monitor.

"Can you open the folder?" she asked. "I want to see the photos."

Nick double-clicked the file and took a step back. A dozen thumbnails of photos filled the screen.

"There's a few hundred pictures in there if you scroll down," he said. "Why don't you look through them? Take your time. I've got—uh—work to do over in the next room. Come get me when you're done."

For the next hour, Emily looked at Nick's photos one by one.

She saw Sara sitting on a mountaintop at dusk, her light brown hair dark with shadows.

Sara in a Ferris wheel car at an amusement park, smiling wider than Emily had even thought possible as the city's lights glimmered in the background.

Sara doing a cartwheel at the beach.

Sara towering over a bowl filled with thirty-two scoops of ice cream, a huge spoon in hand, her mouth open wide as if prepared to swallow everything whole.

Sara grabbing a snowman by his carrot nose.

Sara on the beach, covered in sand shaped to look like a mermaid's tail.

Sara asleep on an unfamiliar couch.

Sara curled up against Nick, nuzzling into his chest.

Emily was crying again now—she'd been crying so much lately—but this time, she realized, they were happy tears. Sara hadn't been the Machine at all. She'd been a girl, just like Emily, a girl who sneaked out and saw her boyfriend and lived a happy life. And in the end, her name on the leaderboard hadn't survived, but these photos had. For the first time in her life, Emily felt like she actually knew her sister.

After she'd looked over the last photo, one of Sara sitting on a picnic blanket on a sunny day in the park, Emily closed the window, got up, and walked over to the next room to find Nick waiting for her.

As he rose from the desk where he'd been sitting, Emily approached him and hugged him close. With her arms around him like this, Nick felt skeletal and frail, and Emily hoped she wasn't hurting him. He hugged her back.

"Thank you," she said, "for introducing me to her."

That night, Emily got home later than usual. After saying good-bye to Nick, she'd skipped the usual run home in favor of a long walk so that she'd have some time to think. So much had been coming at her over the last few weeks that she'd had no time to step back and take it all into consideration.

She'd felt like a juggler asked to deal with ten, twenty, and then thirty bowling pins, so that at some point she wasn't even sure how many were in the air. Now it was time to let the pins drop to the ground and pick up only the ones she cared about.

She could see now that she'd given up too much to be a swimmer. She'd spent so much of her life unhappy, trying to please her father—and also trying to live up to her sister's legacy, one that had turned out to be a lie.

Sara had proved that you could be a record-setting athlete while still living a full life, albeit in secret. In the end, she'd died too early, but it had been an accident, something that could have happened to anyone. Emily couldn't go on living her life based on a random car crash. Sara was dead. Nothing would change that. But Emily was alive, and it was up to her—her and no one else—to build the kind of life she wanted.

"I'm not going." Emily said it looking right across the dinner table at her father, daring him to blink first. The family had gathered around the table to make sugar-free, flaxseed-infused gingerbread cookies, the only holiday treat Emily was traditionally allowed to eat.

"Going where?" asked her mother, pressing a snowman-shaped cookie cutter into some rolled-out dough.

"To Junior Nationals." Emily, favoring a knife over the cookie cutters, was carving out a girl in a pretty dress.

"You're not going?" asked her dad. And then louder. "You're not *going*?!"

"Oh, so you *can* hear me from time to time." Emily finished carving the hem of the dress. Not bad. Maybe if she stopped swimming, she could take up baking.

"Since you were old enough to walk—even before that— you've been swimming, trying to win races," said her dad, pressing a Christmas-tree-shaped cookie cutter angrily into his dough. "And now you're not *going*?"

Emily took a bite of raw dough, then slowly and deliberately started rolling out a fresh sheet before responding.

"You were the one who didn't come to practice today," she said. "You said it was over."

"I was *hoping* you'd redouble your efforts!" he shouted as he stood. "Usually when someone tells you that you can't do something, people in *this* family react by proving them wrong. I remember telling Sara once that she should just give up. She wouldn't get out of the pool until I practically fished her out with a cleaning net!"

"Right," said Emily, mashing a snowflake-shaped cookie cutter over and over into her dough. "Because Sara was your perfect daughter, right? Never broke the rules. Never did anything wrong."

"That's right!" he said. "She didn't argue. She didn't break her regimen. She didn't waste her time sneaking around with boys when she should have been sleeping!"

"Do you really believe that?" asked Emily. She kept mashing down the cookie cutter, pressing overlapping shapes over each other, so that her dough was nearly shredded. "Really. I'm curious. Because I want to know if you're just lying to me, or if you're also lying to yourself."

"What are you talking about?"

For a moment, Emily looked away from him and at the empty chair that had once been Sara's. For the first time she could remember, her sister's absence didn't physically sting her.

"I talked to Nick Brown today," she said, putting the cookie cutter down. "He showed me photos—"

"How dare you bring up that boy's name in my house!"

"I'll say his name all I want, Dad! Now tell me. Did you know?"

"I didn't want you to think of her like that," he said, his voice shaking. "Better that you saw her at her best—"

"—than the way she really was?" Emily finished his sentence.

"That boy—" he started, his voice growing firmer, angrier.

"Nick's not the villain here. No one is. You know what the truth is? There was a terrible accident. And now Sara's dead. But I'm not. And I'm tired of you using some imaginary version of Sara as an excuse to ruin my life. So I'm not going to Junior Nationals. I'm going to homecoming. And if that means you can't be my coach anymore, that's okay. Maybe that's even for the best."

Emily's dad turned to her mom.

"Are you hearing this? She obviously won't listen to me. Maybe you can reason with her."

"Paul," she said. "She *is* being reasonable."

"Great. So now you're taking her side."

"Our deal has always been that you can push the girls as hard as you want—because this is their dream, too. But it sounds like this isn't Emily's dream anymore. We always promised each other we'd never be *those* parents, living out our dreams through our daughters."

"She's fifteen!" Emily's dad shouted. "She doesn't know what she wants!"

"Yes, I do," said Emily. "I want this to be over. I just want a normal life with boys and friends, and staying out past ten at night, and if that means giving up swimming—"

"I won't lose another daughter!" he shouted, his voice beginning to shake again. "I won't. Don't you get it? She lied to us, Em. She stayed out with that boy, and look what happened. I can't lose you the same way."

For the first time since Sara's funeral, Emily could see tears in his eyes.

"Dad, we all miss Sara," said Emily, fighting to keep her own voice steady. "But what happened to her was an accident. And I'm sorry if you can't accept it, but that's how it happened. It was no one's fault. But it's not an excuse to ruin my life, too. I'm out, Dad. I'm done with it. The training, the diet, the swimming. All of it."

"Fine," he said, turning away. "You've made your choice,

Em. Just don't expect to come crawling back to me, asking me to be your coach, when you realize what you've thrown away."

He left the room, and Emily and her mother sat quietly at the table as they heard him stomping up the stairs.

"Mom," said Emily, "I'm sorry. I didn't mean to—"

But before she could say another word, her mother had come over and was hugging her close, just as she had when Emily was younger.

"You have nothing to be sorry for," her mom said. "You know how your father can be. He's like you, entirely stubborn. But give him a day or two, and he'll see the light." She stroked Emily's hair and kissed the top of her head. "Now tell me, who's this boy who's taking you to the dance?"

The next morning, as Emily spied on him from behind a nearby classroom, Ben Kale walked slowly down the hall. The usual bounce had gone out of his step, and his perpetual smile had been replaced with a blank stare. As he got to his locker, he found Spencer waiting for him.

"Dude," said Spencer. "Dude! You'll never guess who I'm taking to homecoming."

Homecoming. The very word made Ben cringe.

"Who?"

"Lindsay, man! Apparently she's been mad crushing on me all year! She's into my bod, naturally. I just wish I'd known sooner, you know? Then I wouldn't have wasted so much time on Dominique."

"Yeah," said Ben distractedly. "Sure."

"I know, I know! I mean, I think maybe Lindsay started liking me so much *because* I was just going after Dom and ignoring her, right? Girls are totally like that. I can't believe it. I totally gamed her without even meaning to!"

Spencer raised his hand for a high five, but Ben ignored it, opening his locker. When he did, a bouquet of roses fell out and landed at his feet. Ben knelt down to pick them up.

"Is there a note?" asked Spencer. "Who are they from?"

"Who do you think?" asked Emily, stepping out from the doorway of the classroom.

"You broke into my locker?" asked Ben, smiling.

"Compared to swimming a fifty-meter backstroke in under twenty-nine seconds, breaking into your locker was easy."

"Spence, give us a minute," said Ben.

"Sure thing," Spencer said with a wink.

As Spencer took off down the hall, he shot them a double thumbs-up.

"Thanks for the roses," said Ben. "They're pretty—and unexpected."

"My mom helped me pick them out."

"How nice of her."

"So, I heard this rumor that your terrible ex-girlfriend may have dumped you, and that now you don't have a homecoming date."

Ben shrugged. "You know how rumors are. Truth is, she's not as bad as everyone says. In fact, I might still kind of like her."

"So if she were, hypothetically, to ask you to the dance—"

"Hypothetically?"

In answer, she leaned forward and kissed him, pressing him up against his locker. She hadn't planned to. But it was something she had to do. Clearly Ben hadn't prepared, either. His lips were tight at first, and his face was scratchy with two-day-old stubble. After a second, though, his lips relaxed and turned soft against hers, and she could feel him there, entirely present, his whole essence concentrated in his mouth against hers.

"Emily," he said, "I—I thought you wanted to wait for, you know, the right moment."

She smiled. "I did."

"So then—we're going to the dance?"

She leaned in once again and kissed him softly. "You've got yourself a date."

Emily and Ben weren't the only couple to get together just in time for homecoming. In the locker room after school that day, Samantha stopped by the bench where Emily was changing and told her she was going to the dance with Nick Brown.

"Just as friends," she added. "He told me that the two of you got a chance to talk about a few things the other day. That's good. I figure it's senior year. Time to let go of some old grudges. Of course, you're just a freshman. I guess you're three years ahead of the game."

"That's sweet," said Emily. "I'm happy for you guys."

"Cool. Anyway, I'd better get changed. Hey, aren't you usually already in your swimsuit by now? What gives?"

"I'm not on such a tight schedule anymore. It's time for me to start changing with the rest of you."

"Cool," said Samantha, opening her locker. "Well, I'll see you out in the pool."

For the first time in weeks, Emily's arms and legs didn't ache as she swam. She'd gotten to bed early the night before, after talking things out with her mom, and instead of tossing and turning as she worried about her messed-up life, she'd gone to sleep the moment her head touched the pillow. She'd woken up this morning feeling lucid and rested for the first time since she'd started her late-night dates with Ben.

As she swam up and down the length of the pool, she realized that for the first time in a long time, she was actually enjoying it.

When she got home that night, Emily walked into her room to find her computer on her desk, just as if it had never left. Sitting next to it was a brand-new phone.

"I, uh, may have taken my frustrations out on your old one," said her dad. "Sorry about that."

"You're apologizing for giving me a new phone?"

He rubbed the small bald spot at the back of his head and looked at his shoes.

"Look, Em. Your mother and I have been talking, and I guess you could say—I guess you could say I overreacted.

Don't get me wrong, it kills me seeing you give up on our dream like this. Really kills me. But it has to be *our* dream. It's like your mom said. I can't relive my swimming days through you."

"So, we're okay?"

He walked toward her and gave her an awkward one-arm hug. It was a start.

"I should probably hit the hay," he said. "But you—you go to sleep when you want. Not after midnight or anything, but it doesn't have to be ten thirty anymore. We can be—flexible."

"Thanks, Dad."

"Oh, I, uh, almost forgot," he said. He brought his left arm around from behind his back to reveal that it was draped with shimmering blue fabric: her dress.

A surge of happiness filled Emily's chest, and a smile broke out on her face.

"I thought you would have torn it to shreds," she said.

"I wanted to. Your mother practically pried it out of my hands." He hesitated for a moment, then added, "I have to confess, I'm still hoping you'll be wearing a swimsuit instead of this on the day in question."

Emily shook her head and didn't say a word.

"No permanent damage done, I hope."

He handed her the dress, and she examined it closely, looking for ripped fabric, but no, the dress was fine. Not even so much as a loose thread.

"'Night, kiddo," he said, and left, closing the door behind him.

Later that night, a few minutes after eleven o'clock, Emily booted up her computer and found Kimi online. They still hadn't spoken since their argument outside the cafeteria.

> *EmilyK14:* Hey...
> *ChEnigma22:* You're up late.
> *EmilyK14:* Yeah. Things have kind of changed around here.
> *EmilyK14:* And I've changed.
> *EmilyK14:* And I'm sorry.
> *EmilyK14:* I was a bad friend. I put myself first. I didn't listen when you tried to tell me what was going on with you.
> *EmilyK14:* But I really miss you now.... And I promise, promise, promise to do better if you'll be my best friend again.
> *ChEnigma22:* Aw, Em.
> *ChEnigma22:* All you had to say was "sorry." (But I DO appreciate the groveling!) Of course we're still best friends!
> *ChEnigma22:* And...I guess I'm just in a forgiving mood today. Since I got a new homecoming date!
> *EmilyK14:* No way! Who?

ChEnigma22: Well...

ChEnigma22: Don't laugh. Or at least don't type lol if you do. But...

ChEnigma22: Remember Kevin Delucca?

EmilyK14: You're kidding, right? Isn't he best friends with Amir? The one who forwarded your rating sheets to the whole school?

ChEnigma22: I know, I know... But then he sent me this really nice e-mail about how bad he felt, and how Amir felt really bad, too.

ChEnigma22: And then they even hacked that Facebook group about me and changed it to 50 Reasons Why Kimi Chen Is Actually Pretty Cool. And he'd noticed I'd written "actually kind of cute" in the pro column of his spreadsheet.

EmilyK14: You did?!

ChEnigma22: There's no accounting for taste I guess... He was one of my lowest-rated suitors...

ChEnigma22: But we just hung out at the mall yesterday and he turned out to be pretty cool. I guess sometimes the numbers lie.

EmilyK14: So in that case... homecoming double date?! I'm sure I can get Ben to go for it.

ChEnigma22: OMG! You and Ben are back together! Em! Congrats!

ChEnigma22: And a double date sounds perfect. I can't wait!

The day before homecoming, Mr. McBride asked Emily to stay after class. That usually wasn't a good sign, but this time a hint of a smile on her teacher's face let Emily know she didn't need to dread this conversation.

"I'm afraid I have some alarming news for you," Mr. McBride announced as Emily approached his desk after the bell rang. Unlike most days, he actually looked up from an essay he'd begun grading. "Your most recent test has thrown off my entire grading curve, thus forcing me to award it an A-plus instead of my usual maximum grade of a simple A."

"I'm—sorry?" Emily *had* studied extra hard, and it certainly made things easier that she wasn't falling asleep on top of her test sheet.

"As am I!" said Mr. McBride. "Should this trend continue, my reputation as the school's harshest grader may be at stake."

He handed her the test.

"I've been informed through certain faculty back channels that you have 'found' your textbook. I trust you'll take better care of it this time?"

"Believe me, I will," said Emily.

Mr. McBride returned to grading the essay.

"That will be all, Ms. Kessler."

Emily backed out of the room, unable to contain her smile.

On the afternoon of homecoming, Kimi came over so that she and Emily could get ready together. Kimi had found a bottle of nail polish that perfectly matched Emily's dress, and they painted her fingernails for the first time. As her nails were drying, Emily wiggled her fingers happily and watched as Kimi painted her own toenails bright red.

They were about to move on to their hair when Emily's dad walked in. He was dressed in his gray game-day suit and wore his lucky coach's whistle—the one he reserved for state and national meets—around his neck.

"I just wanted to say good-bye," he said. "Have fun at the dance. We'll sure miss you at the tournament. Without you around, Dominique won't have much competition."

A little pang of guilt struck at Emily. There was a part of her that wanted to go with him. But the part of her that wanted to see Ben all dressed up, to sway with him on the dance floor and kiss him again, was stronger.

"Thanks for understanding," she said, giving her dad a hug, and when she drew back, she saw that a bit of blue nail polish had somehow ended up on his cheek. She smiled.

"What is it?"

"Nothing," she said. "Good luck at Junior Nationals."

"You're skipping a meet?" Kimi asked as he left.

"Right," said Emily. "To go to the dance."

"You really have changed, Em," said Kimi. "I like it." She

picked up a massive can of hair spray and a curling iron. "Now it's time to get pretty."

Ben couldn't stop staring. The blue dress flowed around Emily's body like water, so that she almost seemed to be swimming instead of walking. For the first time, she felt as graceful on land as she did in the pool. Trying not to stare at her body, Ben took one of Emily's long brown curls in his fingers and bounced it playfully in the air.

"Hey!" said Kimi. "That took, like, an hour to get right. Don't go messing it up in the first ten minutes. You'll have plenty of time for that later."

The three of them, along with Kevin Delucca, who was wearing a T-shirt with a *picture* of a tuxedo on it, much to Kimi's embarrassment, all sat in Ben's car as they drove to the dance.

Ben still couldn't take his eyes off Emily.

"Shouldn't you be, you know, watching the road?" asked Kimi.

"I thought you were supposed to be the one freaking out about my driving, Emily," said Ben, finally looking forward again.

Emily considered that for a second. "I guess I just—forgot."

In truth, she was too entranced by Ben to think about anything else. In place of the pink seventies-style suit he'd threatened over the last few days to wear, he'd worn a simple black one with a white shirt and a blue tie that almost perfectly matched her dress. She suspected that Kimi might have tipped him off. Best of all, he smelled like he had that day he'd first run into her in the cafeteria and called her Yogurt—like vanilla and cookies.

"What's that cologne?" she finally broke down and asked.

"It's not cologne," he said. "It's the artificial flavor they use to make Mrs. Jenkins Holiday Cookies. Just one of the fringe benefits of having a workaholic scientist for a father. Technically, his job is to design custom scents and flavors for mass-produced food."

Emily smiled. Apparently she still had a lot to learn about Ben.

Inside the Twin Branches gym, where homecoming was always held, the four of them headed straight for the dance floor and joined a small circle from Ben's crowd, including Zach and Hannah, Spencer and Lindsay, and Hector and Amanda. A fast song with a driving bass rattled the windows and hurt Emily's ears.

"Good to see you!" Hannah shouted over the music. "I'm so glad you and Ben are back together."

In the meantime, Lindsay was looking at Kimi, horrified. It didn't take Emily too long to see why: They were wearing the same dress.

"This can't be happening," said Lindsay. "I—I'm dressed just like the *Realtor.*"

"And I'd have to say she's pulling it off better," said Kevin, smiling at Kimi. She gave his hand a thankful squeeze as Lindsay ran for the girls' room.

Heading back from the snack table by herself a few minutes later, Emily spotted Samantha and Nick talking in the corner. As she passed them, Samantha giggled at something, and Emily smiled. It was the first time she'd heard Samantha laugh.

Away from the circle on the dance floor, Kevin and Kimi were now talking with Amir and an incredibly tall, black-haired girl who was pronouncing all of her *o*'s as *ooo*. As she walked by them, Emily overheard her say, "Of *course* we have homecoming back in Canada!" Emily shook her head in disbelief. So Amir really *did* have a hot Canadian girlfriend.

Nearby, Cameron Clark stood alone. Seeing Emily, he walked over and looked down at her, his eyes staring deep into hers.

"Where's your date?" he asked, and she pointed out Ben in the center of the dance floor, talking loudly to Spencer over the music.

"Where's yours?"

He shrugged.

"I came alone. Figured I might meet someone here at the dance. Maybe you'd like to—"

He put a hand on her shoulder, and his touch was like fire on her skin—in a good way, but Ben was waiting. Emily felt the sudden need to shake Cameron off—to push him away.

"I—I better get back to my date," she said, retreating from him, and he nodded.

"Of course."

She walked away quickly, wondering what had just

happened between them. She hoped Ben hadn't noticed. After a few worried minutes, though, she decided to put it out of her mind. Whatever she felt toward Cameron Clark, she'd worry about it some other day.

Today was about concentrating on the good things. A few months ago, she might have been haunted by the knowledge that this would have been Sara's senior-year homecoming, but it seemed okay now, as if her ghost was finally at rest.

Lost in the music, Emily was slow-dancing with Ben near Kimi and Kevin, when he said, "You know, I'm really glad you made me come. The music is good, my friends all came, and I'm here with the prettiest girl at school. If you had told me a couple of months ago that I'd be here, I would have laughed. Now I never want to leave."

"You know, I've heard that the winter formal's coming up," said Emily. "And then prom after that."

"Very interesting," said Ben. "I guess I'll have to keep my grades up. You're sure you're not just a secret agent sent here by my dad to make sure I get into a good college, right?"

"What do you think?"

She leaned in and kissed him softly on the lips. It felt so natural now. How had she ever lived without it?

"Looks like Dominique decided not to show," he said as the next song started. "Good thing—honestly, I was a little worried there would be some drama between the two of you."

Emily hadn't said a word to Ben about Junior Nationals. Better just to let him enjoy the dance with her instead of letting him know what she'd given up. Mentioning it would only have been selfish.

"Yeah," she said. "I'm glad Dom's not here."

"Of course she's not," said Kimi from a few feet over. "She's at the Junior Nationals."

Cringe. Thanks for nothing, Kimi.

Ben took a step away from Emily and looked her in the eye.

"What's she talking about?"

"It's Junior Nationals today—but I decided I'd rather be here."

"So you don't want to be there?"

"No," she said. "I mean yes. I guess so. But not as much as I want to be here."

"Emily—" He didn't take his eyes off her once. "You're incredibly sweet, skipping that for me. But I—I couldn't live with myself if I let you throw away everything you've been working so hard for, just for my sake."

"Well, it's not just for you. This is about me being able to make my own choices, even if it means occasionally sacrificing something I want."

He kept looking into her eyes as if trying to read her mind.

"What time are you scheduled to swim?"

"My first race is at eight."

"It's seven-oh-four right now," said Kimi. "And the meet is over in Las Playas. That's an hour away."

Ben looked around the dance and nodded.

"You know, I *told* you this dance was going to be lame," he said, arching an eyebrow. "I say we bail and take a little road trip."

"But you just said you never wanted to leave!"

"Really? That doesn't sound like something I'd say."

"You'd really leave early like this, for me?"

"Are you kidding?" he asked. "I've thrown better parties in my sleep. Literally. I've gone to sleep in the middle of lots of my parties."

"You know, I've always wanted to go to Las Playas," said Kimi.

"And where she goes, I go," said Kevin. "Who knows when she'll mark a whole bunch of demerits in my cons column and dump me for someone better?"

"Jerk. You know I stopped doing that!"

"Emily," said Ben, "what do you say? It's up to you. Feel like a swim?"

For a moment, Emily imagined seven girls standing up on blocks at the side of the pool while the center lane—her lane—was left vacant. She imagined Dominique swimming out ahead of everyone else and smiling triumphantly as she won the race. She imagined all the names on the leaderboard disappearing, replaced with Dominique's. Emily tightened her hands into fists.

"Let's do this."

"That's what I wanted to hear," said Ben. "You have exactly two minutes to grab your stuff from your locker and meet me at the front door. You've got a race to win."

Fifteen minutes later, Emily was naked under a blanket in the back of Ben's car. Okay, it wasn't as bad as it sounded. In order to change, she'd had to strip off her homecoming dress in transit, and was now slipping on her swimsuit. Kimi sat in the back with her, holding the blanket over her and making sure the guys didn't peek.

The funny thing was, Emily barely felt embarrassed. In just a few weeks, she'd come a long way from worrying about Dominique's teasing in the locker room.

"After all the time we spent picking out that dress," said Kimi sadly.

"Could you hand me my swim cap?" asked Emily from under the blanket.

"Your hair! Your curls! We didn't even take a picture."

"It's like you said at the start of the year. The winter formal isn't too far away. And then there's prom after that."

"Oooh. Good point! I've already got some ideas for your hair next time. What would you say to a Snooki-style pouf?"

"Um, we'll talk about it," said Emily as she stuffed her carefully done hair under her swim cap.

"Shouldn't you be going a little faster?" Kevin asked Ben in the front seat. "You're doing *exactly* the speed limit."

"I'm just playing it safe," said Ben.

"Yeah," said Kevin. "But according to the map on my phone, that means we're going to get there at eight-oh-two."

"He's got a point, Ben," said Emily. "Just a few miles over the speed limit wouldn't hurt."

"Are you sure?" he asked.

She pulled the blanket aside and saw his smile in the rear-view mirror.

"One or two miles over the limit wouldn't hurt."

At exactly seven fifty-seven, the car reached the Las Playas Country Club pool, and Emily and Kimi hopped out. The guys would park the car and meet them inside.

"Good luck in there!" shouted Ben as Emily ran for the door.

A minute and a half later, the girls entered the main swimming facility, where hundreds of fans sat on the bleachers, looking down at dozens of the best swimmers from around the country.

Where the Spartan Academy swimming facility had been sleek and ultramodern, Las Playas was classical, the pools shining sparkling white and lined with marble. The surrounding stands were laid out in a gigantic circle, like the Colosseum, around pools arranged in a four-square formation. Walking in, Emily felt like a gladiator. A gladiator who had shown up just in the nick of time.

"Emily!" Before she even saw him, her dad was picking her up in a huge bear hug. "I knew you'd come!"

"You did? Because I just realized it about fifty-eight minutes ago."

"Better late than never," he said. "Or maybe better on time than late? Anyway, the point is, the first race is about to start. You've got the fifty-meter backstroke in pool three. The meet is running about five minutes behind schedule, so you should have just enough time to stretch out."

She had to start with the 50-meter backstroke? In which Dominique now held the national record? *Perfect*, she thought. *At least this way I can get my first loss out of the way early.*

"What's with the frown?" asked Ben, winded from sprinting in from the parking lot. "Should I not have brought you?"

"I'm just not looking forward to losing this one."

"So don't lose. I was there at the match against Wilson when you beat Dominique in every race. Who says you can't do it again?"

"She's better now than she was then."

He put his hands on her shoulders. "So are you."

"It's true, Em!" said Kimi. "You were pushing yourself way too hard for months. You were exhausted when she beat you. Now you've actually caught up on sleep."

"*All fifty-meter backstroke participants, please report to pool three!*" boomed a voice from overhead.

"You've got this, Emily," said Ben. "You can do it."

"Kick her pretty blond butt!" shouted Kimi.

Her dad gave her a silent nod.

Emily saw Dominique before Dominique saw her. She clung to the edge of the pool, her goggles already fastened, chanting her victory mantra. She didn't break out of her trance until Emily splashed down in the lane next to her.

"Kessler?" she asked, her concentration clearly broken. "Are you wearing makeup?"

Emily touched her hand to her face, then looked at her fingertips and found them covered in running mascara.

"Consider it war paint," she said.

"I heard you weren't coming."

"You heard wrong."

"Not that it matters," said Dominique. "You're yesterday's news anyway. Or haven't you heard? *Swimmer's Monthly* is doing a follow-up article, all about me. Apparently they just weren't interested in you anymore."

Emily fastened her goggles. "Then I'll have to give them something to write about." Emily clutched the underside of her starting block, and as she lifted her body slightly above the water, it felt almost weightless. She concentrated everything on the echoing voices above her as she waited for the sound of the starting horn.

When it blared, she was ready. She pushed off the wall and immediately went into her stroke. Nothing in her body hurt this time, and the movement felt effortless. Before she even knew it, she'd reached the far wall and was starting her turn. As she pushed off again, she caught a glimpse of Dominique to her left. They were dead even.

She reached back now with everything she had. On her periphery, she could sense Dominique matching her stroke for stroke. And then, just as they were about to reach the wall, Emily felt as if a pair of unseen hands were pushing her forward, helping to carry her those last few feet.

Maybe it was just her imagination, and she would never tell anyone about it, but in that moment she opened her eyes and saw her sister's face. She was about to say Sara's name when she felt her fingers touch the wall.

She tore off her goggles and looked up at the times on the leaderboard. She saw Dominique's time first: 28.0 seconds, just like last time. Dominique had matched her own national record.

Except that it wasn't a national record anymore. A few inches up, next to Emily's name, was the number 27.9.

"Ladies and gentlemen," echoed the announcer's voice. "For the second time in just a little more than two weeks, we have a new national record. Congratulations to Emily Kessler!"

As Emily pulled herself from the pool, her dad ran over to wrap her in a towel and give her a congratulatory hug. All around them, camera flashes erupted from the bleachers, capturing her triumph. The night was far from over—there would be a lot more races to come. But in this moment, she had won, and for the first time in years, she smiled for the cameras.

ACKNOWLEDGMENTS

Many thanks to the *Surviving High School* writing team, who provided invaluable feedback through the creative process: Eric Dean, Royal McGraw, Andrew Shvarts, and Jennifer Young.

Thanks also to everyone at Electronic Arts who believed in this book and helped make it happen, especially Rob Simpson, Pat O'Brien, and Oliver Miao.

I'm very grateful, also, to our team at Little, Brown: Erin Stein, Pam Gruber, and Mara Lander. Thanks for all your hard work on behalf of our book!

Finally, thanks most of all to Kara Loo, writing team leader, editor, and fiancée extraordinaire.

★★★★★★★★★★★★★★★★★★★★★★★★★★

Don't miss the second book in the
Surviving High School series,

HOW TO BE A STAR

Tired of playing the sidekick to her swimming-superstar best friend, Kimi Chen feels it's time to step into the spotlight and secure her own place at the coveted center table of the cafeteria. But when a low-budget music video she made hits the Web and goes viral, forget about being just popular–Kimi is *famous*! Boys want to date her, girls want to be her, and she is even asked to perform on her favorite television show. Things are finally looking up! What could possibly go wrong?

Find out how Kimi's stars align

May 2013.

BOB500

★★★★★★★★★★★★★★★★★★★★★★★★★